GREEK'S BRIDE BY BLACKMAIL

JACKIE ASHENDEN

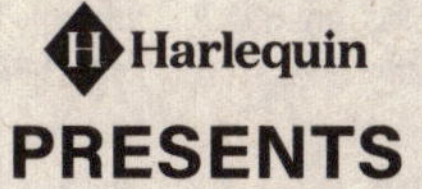

PRESENTS

Recycling programs for this product may not exist in your area.

ISBN-13: 978-1-335-61402-5

Greek's Bride by Blackmail

For questions and comments about the quality of this book, please contact us at CustomerService@Harlequin.com.

Harlequin Enterprises ULC
22 Adelaide St. West, 41st Floor
Toronto, Ontario M5H 4E3, Canada
www.Harlequin.com

HarperCollins Publishers
Macken House, 39/40 Mayor Street Upper,
Dublin 1, D01 C9W8, Ireland
www.HarperCollins.com

Printed in Lithuania

1 2 3 4 5 6 7 8 9 10 LIT 28 27 26 25

He remained expressionless as he slid the ring onto her finger.

It was a plain gold band, nothing fancy, though there was another surprise in that he'd got one for himself too.

She put it on his finger in return, this time steadfastly avoiding his gaze as she let go of his long, blunt fingers. She didn't want to meet it, which felt too much like surrender for her comfort.

The priest intoned the rest of the ceremony, pronouncing them husband and wife, and then that Archimedes may kiss his new bride.

Zoe didn't expect that he would, so it came as yet another huge shock when those long fingers suddenly gripped her chin, tipping her face up, and his mouth brushed hers in the most featherlight and fleeting of kisses. She froze. It was as if someone had hit her over the back of the head with something heavy, making her dizzy and her thought processes sluggish.

All she could think was that Archimedes had kissed her. He had *kissed* her. And the worst part of it was that, even though it had been the briefest of kisses, she could somehow feel it *everywhere*.

Jackie Ashenden writes dark, emotional stories with alpha heroes who've just gotten the world to their liking only to have it blown apart by their kick-ass heroines. She lives in Auckland, New Zealand, with her husband, the inimitable Dr. Jax, two kids and two rats. When she's not torturing alpha males and their gutsy heroines, she can be found drinking chocolate martinis, reading anything she can lay her hands on, wasting time on social media or being forced to go mountain biking with her husband. To keep up-to-date with Jackie's new releases and other news, sign up to her newsletter at jackieashenden.com.

Books by Jackie Ashenden

Harlequin Presents

Spanish Marriage Solution
Newlywed Enemies
King, Enemy, Husband
His Forced Sicilian Bride
Heir with My Enemy

Scandalous Heirs

Italian Baby Shock
The Twins That Bind

Work Wives to Billionaires' Wives

Boss's Heir Demand

Captured and Claimed

Christmas Eve Ultimatum
His Heir of Revenge

Visit the Author Profile page
at Harlequin.com for more titles.

GREEK'S BRIDE BY BLACKMAIL

Thanks to Oliver Twist, Anakin Skywalker
and a hint of Demon Copperhead

CHAPTER ONE

Archimedes Athineos was not used to waiting, and today, as the hour of his marriage approached, he was even less inclined to do so. However, Banks had been clear. If he did not go through with this ridiculous farce of a wedding, Banks would release information to the authorities that would put Archimedes behind bars, and for years.

If Archimedes hated waiting in general, waiting in a jail cell would be infinitely worse, and he didn't doubt that Banks would and could do exactly as he promised. Archimedes had, after all, got his own ruthlessness from somewhere, and that somewhere was the man who'd brought him up as a child, along with several other children he'd also fostered.

Banks was a modern-day Fagin, his shabby house in London full of the latest high-tech, the kids he fostered taught how to be elite hackers, stealing money from the rich and giving to the poor—at least, that was what he'd always told them. The poor being him.

Archimedes—arguably Banks's best pupil—had got out as soon as he'd turned eighteen, and had immediately begun accumulating money by whatever means necessary. Money was power, and since Archimedes had never had any power, that was what he wanted.

These days, money and power were all he had. He was CEO and owner of Ares Security, a huge security company that not only dealt with online security for banks and hospitals, but also for governments and the military.

It had taken him some years to get to this point, and his past was chequered to say the least, but here he was and while waiting in this little church deep in the City of London was the last place he wanted to be, and Banks the last person he wanted to see, he had no choice.

He *hated* having no choice.

One day he was going to take Banks down, but until he was able to secure the dirt that Banks had on him, he was forced to accede to his foster father's wishes.

Which apparently included marriage.

Banks hadn't said who he was marrying—another 'pleasant' surprise—only that he must get married and remain with his wife for a year. Oh, and also, a baby would be required.

Archimedes glanced one more time at his two-hundred-thousand-dollar watch, the seconds slipping by, and gritted his teeth.

It was a small, historic and very pretty church, but Archimedes was interested in neither its prettiness nor its historical value. It was cold, and Banks had yet to appear, and he was not amused. Archimedes found little amusing except for making money, and since this wasn't related to money, he was even more impatient than he normally was. Which wasn't very.

He was just on the point of calling his recalcitrant foster father when the church doors opened and Banks came in. He was in his customary three-piece suit, his grey hair and beard still as long and as wild as Archimedes remembered, and his weathered face broke into a smile as he saw his erstwhile foster son standing by the altar.

'Archie,' he said expansively, coming over to Archimedes, his arms wide in the expectation of a hug.

Archimedes, whose experience of being fostered by Banks was not a happy one, made no move. Instead, he drew himself up to his considerable height and demanded, 'What is this all about?'

Banks dropped his arms. 'I haven't seen you for fifteen years and that's the first thing you say to me? Not the way I brought you up, lad.'

'You didn't bring me up,' Archimedes said in frigid tones, disliking intensely being called 'lad'. 'I brought myself up. Answer the goddamn question.'

Banks's fake smile vanished, a calculating expression taking its place. 'So we're going to play it this way, are we? Fine. You know what it's all about. I told you in my email. I want you to marry the woman of my choice, live with her for a year and conceive a child. That's all. A mere bagatelle, dear boy.'

Archimedes hadn't forgotten his foster father's tendency to make very complicated things sound easy. Or the punishments he meted out when the complicated thing wasn't done to his specifications.

Banks was ruthless, hiding his vicious streak behind an easy, fatherly smile. Archimedes did not hide his. His vicious streak was out in the open for everyone to see, as was his ruthlessness.

'Why?' he snapped.

Banks waved an airy hand. 'Oh... I'm getting on in years and I would like a son or daughter to bring up as my own. Also, there's the little question of my business and who I'd pass it on to.' He said this as if he was talking about wanting scones with his tea, not about a child.

Archimedes had no desire for children. His own childhood had consisted of being abandoned by his mother, who'd left Greece for London to escape from her violent husband, and then left London to escape from Archimedes. He'd gone straight into the foster system at the age of five and after being bounced from one home to another, he was then fostered with Banks at seven. He'd learned how to hack into any computer system by the age of ten, and by twelve was stealing money and information like a professional more than twice his age.

As to marriage, he had no desire for that either. Love was alien to him, and the thought of sharing his worldly goods with another person was anathema.

Still, marrying some woman and giving Banks a child to bring up was better than going to prison.

Archimedes was not in the habit of thinking too deeply about matters that didn't either interest or concern him, so he didn't bother thinking too deeply about this one. He had meetings to get to later in the day, and he wanted this bullshit to be over and done with so he could get on with running his business.

'You did have children, if you recall,' he couldn't help pointing out. 'Many of them, in fact.'

'True,' Banks allowed. 'But none I brought up as my own. And all of them leave in the end.' He said this last with a reproving look.

'Maybe if you'd treated us better, we wouldn't have left,' Archimedes said. He'd been Banks's prize, his golden goose, and Banks had done everything in his power to keep Archimedes from leaving. But he'd failed in the end.

Banks shrugged. 'Tough love, my boy. It never hurt anyone.'

Archimedes ignored that. 'I fail to see the need for marriage,' he said. 'Or why you want me to be the father of this child.'

'Because your brain has always been astonishing, Archie, and I want the child to carry the very best genes. As to the marriage, I can hardly have the child born out of wedlock, can I? It has to be legal and all above board.'

Banks's reasoning didn't make much sense to Archimedes but, fundamentally, why all of this was required didn't interest him. He had to do what Banks said regardless of whether it made sense or not, so the why of it didn't matter.

Archimedes glanced at his watch again, irritated by the passing of time. He'd always been an impatient man—there was too much to do and not enough time to do any of it—but he could wait when it suited him.

It didn't suit him now.

'Let's get on with it.' He made no attempt to hide his displeasure. 'I have business to attend to.'

Banks gave him a genial smile. 'Impatient as ever, lad. Seems you haven't changed.'

'Neither have you,' Archimedes said. 'You're the same manipulative, venal bastard you always were.'

Banks inclined his head as if Archimedes had delivered the very finest of compliments. 'Blackmail was the only way to get what I wanted, alas. And in return—'

'In return,' Archimedes interrupted, deciding now was as good a time as any to make his intentions clear, 'you will give me every piece of incriminating evidence you have on me.'

Banks's genial expression remained. 'You're in no position to make demands.'

But Archimedes did not take kindly to being told what to do. He'd engineered his life specifically so he could be in complete control of it, and that did not include being blackmailed and manipulated by his foster father any more.

However, Banks certainly had dirt on him, and he'd sent Archimedes pictures to prove it. Lists of IP addresses, money trails, voice recordings of him discussing hacking into various companies. When Banks had first sent his blackmail email, Archimedes had got in touch with an old contact in the crime underworld to get the evidence off Banks, but the contact was unable to find it.

Banks had hidden it very securely. That all the evidence against Archimedes had been collected when he was only fifteen didn't matter. Neither did the fact that his hacking days were over, and his company was all legal and above board. Even if, by some miracle, the information Banks had on him didn't result in a jail term, it would certainly do irreparable damage to his company if it got out, and there was no way Archimedes could risk that.

There was no way he could leave that evidence with Banks either.

'Since you're the one asking for my biological child, I would say I'm certainly in a position to make demands,' he said. 'Legally, you wouldn't have a leg to stand on if I decided to keep it. And in the meantime, I'll be trying everything in my power to get that evidence from you, and I'm sure you're aware of exactly how much power I have.'

Banks's bright blue eyes narrowed, his expression once again turning calculating—the expression that Archimedes was most familiar with. 'You can try,' he said, but Archimedes caught the slight hint of uncertainty in his voice.

He'd spent years learning how to exploit weaknesses, both in firewalls and in people, and his ability to be quite ruthless about it had been his main driver for the success of his company. So he had no compunction in exploiting Banks's now.

'You don't want to make an enemy of me, Banks,' he said flatly. 'What you want is for me to forget you. So, I ask again. Give me every piece of evidence you have on me, and I will give you the child.'

The old man's gaze narrowed, and he stared at Archimedes for a good minute. 'Very well,' he said at last. 'I was going to keep it for emergency purposes, but I have plenty of evidence on others that I can use should the need arise.'

Archimedes allowed himself a thin smile, since it was, after all, very satisfying out-manipulating the manipulative Banks. 'I will have my lawyers draw up a contract.'

'Oh, really?' Banks looked disapproving. 'Surely we can settle this like gentlemen? With a handshake?'

Archimedes's smile turned savage. 'I'm not a gentleman, Banks. You made sure of that.'

Banks opened his mouth to reply, then the church doors opened, and he smiled instead. 'Ah,' he said with genuine pleasure. 'It appears that your bride has arrived at last.'

Zoe Hargreaves did not want to be here. She *had* to be here. Banks, her foster father, had been very clear when he'd told her what he wanted from her.

Marriage to a man of his choice, whom Zoe would have to live with for a year and conceive a child with. A child who would then be turned over to Banks to bring up. In return she would get all the money she needed to start her own company, so she could finally stop working for him.

It had sounded ludicrous when he'd first told her about it, and now, as she pushed open the church door, preparing to marry a man she'd never met, it didn't seem any less ludicrous.

Especially when she saw who was standing next to Banks at the altar.

Zoe froze in the doorway, feeling as if she'd been punched in the stomach. Hard.

Archimedes. What the hell was *he* doing here?

He'd been the boy she'd grown up with in Banks's house. The boy who'd looked out for her, protected her, kept her from the loneliness that had always threatened to pull her down. The boy whom she'd developed a huge crush on from the time she was eleven, but because he was three years older than her, he'd never even noticed.

He was also the boy who'd abandoned her the moment he'd turned eighteen, leaving her alone in that house with Banks.

She'd never forgiven him for that. Never.

He'd only contacted her once in the fifteen years since he'd been gone, and that was to offer her a position in his new company, but she'd refused. Of course she'd refused. It was too little, too late, and anyway, she wouldn't ever work *for* him. No, she wasn't ever working for anyone again.

The money Banks was offering her would set her up to be her own boss and maybe if Archimedes was very lucky, she might offer *him* a position in her wildly successful company.

She'd followed his career with some reluctance, telling herself it was good to learn all about the competition and not because she wanted to see what he was doing and how he was doing and just to see him. She knew his reputation and that of his company—rigorous, meticulous, their online security systems impregnable and continuously tested to remain that way.

He was brilliant and he always had been, even as a boy, but now…

He was something more.

She took a breath, trying to ignore the cold shock threading through her.

At eighteen he'd been tall and rangy, only a promise of the man he was now. A man who seemed taller, was definitely broader, and who had a presence, a charisma that took up space, filling the tiny church and stealing the breath from her lungs.

He was in a dark suit with a deep blue shirt, his silk tie in a contrasting charcoal, and his bluc stare—the stare she used to dream about at night when she was a lonely teenager—was fixed on her.

He was *so* different. Even the photos she'd seen online didn't do him justice. He used to be a pretty boy, but the man standing by the altar wasn't pretty. His features were hard, tempered like a blade, his black, winged brows giving him a demonic look. Demon, that was what his handle had been years ago, and that was what he looked like now. A beautiful demon sent from the past to taunt her.

Next to him was Banks, whom she'd once thought of as tall, but in comparison with Archimedes, he looked like a child.

'Your bride', that was what Banks had said as she'd pushed open the door. That did not mean what she thought it did, right? It did not mean that she was going to marry Archimedes. It *could* not mean that she was going to marry Archimedes.

Archimedes himself said nothing, his blue gaze utterly expressionless.

She'd once been able to tell what he was thinking. Now, Egyptian hieroglyphics were more readable.

Rearranging her face to show the same absence of expression, she let the door bang shut behind her and walked slowly down the aisle towards the two men.

Banks opened his mouth to speak, but it was Archimedes who said, 'You're late.' His voice was hard, flat, and much deeper than she remembered.

Zoe stopped dead, looking first at him, then at Banks. 'Please tell me that I'm not marrying—'

'Me?' Archimedes finished, raising one of those demonic brows. 'Yes. Apparently, you are.'

Banks started towards her, an apologetic smile on his face. 'Dear girl, I know I should have been clear with you about who you were to marry, but I thought you wouldn't agree to it if I told you it was Archie.'

'Yes,' Zoe said flatly, folding her arms and giving her foster father a stare just as hard as the one Archimedes was giving her. 'You should have. And no, I most certainly wouldn't have agreed.'

Archimedes muttered something under his breath. 'I don't have time for this nonsense,' he said. 'Come here, Zoe, and let's get this over and done with.'

She gave him an incredulous look. 'You haven't seen me for fifteen years and that's the first thing you say?'

Banks held his hands up in a peace gesture. 'Zoe, dear girl, I know this is a shock but—'

'You're damn right it's a shock,' she snapped, turning her fury onto Banks. 'I'm not doing it.'

Banks looked apologetic. 'And if you don't, you don't get the money you need. Quid pro quo, dear girl. You know the drill. You want something, you have to give something.'

Oh, she knew the drill. She knew all too well.

Archimedes only stood there, glancing down at his watch every so often as if he was in the middle of the most boring meeting imaginable and was merely waiting for the moment when he could leave.

She remembered that about him too. Always impatient, could never sit still, wanting to go onto the next thing and then the next. She'd once adored that about him. She'd found being with him like holding a live wire, all sharp, bright shocks of energy that made her feel as if she was as exciting and dangerous and interesting as he was. And when he'd left, he'd taken all that electricity with him, leaving her inert, cold and dead.

'Did Banks tell you?' she demanded. 'That you'd be marrying me?'

'No,' Archimedes said. 'But I don't care who I'm marrying. I have meetings I have to get to this afternoon and I only allowed an hour out of my schedule for this.'

Zoe blinked. 'But you know what Banks has asked—'

'Yes, I do know,' he said, interrupting yet again, another habit she remembered from years ago, because he was always too impatient to wait for people's answers, his brain already firing onto the next thing. 'I don't care about that either.'

'You might not care,' she shot back, unable to help the anger fuelled by shock that flooded through her. 'But I do. I don't want to marry you, or live with you, still less have a kid with you.'

Archimedes lifted one broad shoulder. 'Leave then. It doesn't matter to me.'

Deep inside her, the child she'd once been, the kid who'd been devastated by his abandonment, wanted to shout, *Did I ever matter to you?* But she shoved that kid to the back of her mind.

She wasn't going down that route again. She'd left her childhood crush behind her, along with the rest of her crappy childhood. Archimedes didn't matter to her now.

So why are you making such a fuss? If he doesn't care, then why should you?

A good point. Arguing and being angry made this seem like more of a big deal than it actually was, and she'd spent most of her adulthood making everything less of a big deal than it actually was, so why start now?

'Ah,' Banks said, his gaze going to the doors behind her. 'And here is Father Percy.' He walked past her to greet the priest, who'd just come in.

Zoe stared at Archimedes. 'What did he offer you?' she asked.

'That doesn't matter either,' he said, his tone as expressionless as his face.

'What about the child he wants?' she persisted, because surely he had some thoughts about that.

'What about the child?' That brow rose again. 'We give it to Banks to look after, end of story.'

Something twisted inside her, something she'd been trying very hard not to pay any attention to. It wasn't that she hadn't thought of having kids—she'd come to the decision that she did want them, but only in the context of a family. She didn't want any child of hers to grow up, for example, with Banks as a father. Not that he'd been the worst. He'd been good to her after Archimedes had left, mellowing a lot in his old age, but still.

'You don't have a single thought about that?' She stared at him in disbelief. 'You'd really be happy for a child to be brought up in Banks's house?'

'They will be warm, dry, fed and cared for,' Archimedes said negligently. 'What else does a child need?'

Love, Zoe wanted to say. *A child needs love.* But she knew already that Archimedes wouldn't understand the first thing about love. He never had. She'd told him once about her early experience of growing up with loving parents, and the terrible grief when they'd both been killed in a car accident. But he'd simply shrugged the same way he was shrugging now. No one had ever loved him, he'd told her, yet he was fine. He'd never seen the need for it anyway. Banks was okay. He fed them, gave them a roof over their heads, made sure they had clothes to wear. They wanted for nothing, or at least that was what Archimedes had said.

'To be put to work the moment they turn seven?' She couldn't keep the shock from her tone.

Again that casual shrug. 'Does it matter? We both had the same upbringing and I don't know about you, but Ares Security is vastly successful so really, I couldn't have had a better start in life.'

'You have to be joking,' Zoe said blankly.

'Does it look like I'm joking?' His face was hard, his blue gaze sapphire-sharp, and that something inside Zoe, the thing she never wanted to acknowledge, twisted again.

The priest and Banks approached and Archimedes's razor-sharp gaze shifted. 'Finally,' he said.

Zoe swallowed, her mouth dry. This couldn't be happening, could it? Was she really going to agree to marry Archimedes? And have a child with him?

She'd been wanting to strike out on her own for years, but she hadn't done anything about it yet, because she had complicated feelings about leaving Banks. Memories of her birth parents were few, and she treasured those, but their loss had left a huge hole in her life and it had been Banks who'd filled it, however imperfectly. He'd been a father to her in more ways than one, especially after Archimedes's departure. He'd been kind to her in those lonely months following, and because he was the only family she had, she hadn't been able to bring herself to leave him.

She loved him, in a way. He hadn't been totally awful. He had indeed kept all the kids in his care fed and clothed, and while he didn't send them to school, he did educate them himself, alongside lessons in online crime.

Everyone had eventually grown up and left, though, and most of them he'd let go. She, however, had chosen to stay. He'd often told her how valuable she was to him, and while that wasn't exactly love, it was enough for her.

She'd eventually persuaded him to give up the black hat business and become an online security consultant, so at least he'd stopped his illegal activities. However, he was getting on in years and had no one to look after him, and she couldn't abandon him, not after he'd given her a roof over her head.

Still, if she wanted to finally strike out on her own, she was going to need the money he'd promised her if she went through with this. The salary he paid her was generous and she'd been squirelling away every penny, yet it still wasn't going to be enough to build the company she'd been dreaming about—a service that would help protect people from online scammers, hunt down those responsible for sextortion involving young people and women, and anything else black hat operators did that caused harm and distress. A restitution in a way, to make up for all the illegal things she'd done under Banks's tutelage.

'Zoe,' Archimedes said, his tone sharp as a whip. He snapped his fingers and pointed to the floor beside him. 'Come here. Let's get this done.'

Immediately, she bridled at the command in his voice. 'Don't you dare snap your fingers at me.' She lifted her chin, giving him a furious look. 'I'm not a bloody dog.'

'Are we going to stand around arguing about this all day?' he demanded. 'I've got another half an hour and that's all.'

Despite her determination not to make a drama

of this, Zoe couldn't stand the thought of acquiescing without at least a cursory protest. She didn't like being told what to do, especially by him.

'What about a dress?' She lifted her own brow at him. 'And flowers? I'm a bride, Archimedes. How can I be a bride if I don't have a dress?'

Something glittered in his eyes briefly, a spark of something that oddly made her breath catch. He studied her for one long moment, then took his phone out of his pocket and raised it to his ear. 'Jen? I need a bridal gown delivered to this address within the next ten minutes. Size ten. White silk. Full length and fitted, I think. Oh, and a bouquet of peonies. Make them pink.' He ended the call and put the phone back in his pocket. 'There,' he said. 'Satisfied?'

CHAPTER TWO

ZOE HARGREAVES DID not look satisfied in the least. She looked extremely pissed off, which he supposed she had reason to be.

Clearly, Banks hadn't told her who she was marrying either, and given the expression on her face as she'd entered the church, she wasn't happy about it.

Good. That made two of them.

He'd hidden his shock at her appearance the way he hid every single emotion he'd ever had—under an expressionless mask. In fact, he'd been hiding his emotions for so long that by now it was instinctive to do so. Sometimes he'd even forget he had them, so it came as quite a surprise to find that he still had the capability to be shocked at all.

Nevertheless, he had been. He hadn't thought of her for years, at least not since she'd turned down his offer of a position in his company, a position he'd created especially for her since he'd heard she was still working for Banks, and thought she might need a way out.

He was a little surprised that she'd flatly turned him down, but he hadn't let it bother him. He'd simply got on with his business, pushing both her and the reason she might have said no to him to the back of his mind.

Yet now here she was, standing in front of him, and the sweet, affectionate and loyal little girl he remembered had vanished. In her place was a delicate-looking woman with glossy black hair, a heart-shaped face, a perfect bow of a mouth and grey eyes like a winter storm. And most definitely a woman, that was immediately clear.

She wore jeans, a black T-shirt, a worn-looking black leather jacket and had a capacious leather satchel slung over her shoulder. Not clothes that were inherently sexy or otherwise, but the T-shirt clung to generous breasts and highlighted a neat waist, while her jeans drew attention to the gentle swell of her hips and thighs.

She was beautiful, there was no disputing that. Very beautiful. Not that he'd ever been a man who had his head turned by mere beauty. No, he could get beauty anywhere and very often did, since he had his pick of sexual partners.

He wasn't thinking of Zoe in that way, though. His plan for this marriage was simply to get the ceremony over and done with, then he would ship his bride off to whichever of his many houses she wanted to stay in, and that would be 'living together'. As to the baby, fertility doctors could handle that. They didn't even have to see each other if they didn't want to. And it was plain that Zoe didn't want to.

There was an unexpected and unwanted ache inside him at that thought, but that was just another emotion to dismiss and ignore. He had more important things to think about, such as Zoe arguing with him and prolonging this whole farce unreasonably. Well, she could try, but he wasn't going to let her. If she wanted a bloody gown, then he'd get her a bloody gown. Flowers, too.

'Are you insane?' The anger glittering in her eyes made them glow silver.

He remembered her temper that blew through like a cyclone before vanishing just as quickly as it came. Remembered those sparks that would glitter just like the ones in her eyes now. He used to call her 'Star' because of that glitter, and because once she'd been his North Star.

'Not last time I checked,' he said, unable to help but notice that the flush of temper in her cheeks madc the sparks in her eyes even more apparent.

'You have no idea what size I am, and as for wearing a dress you ordered like you'd order a meal, I'm not—'

'Stop arguing, Zoe,' Archimedes interrupted, his patience rapidly fraying, not that he had much to begin with. 'The quicker we do this, the quicker we can go about our day.'

Tension vibrated in every line of her small figure and her mouth was a hard line, and he found himself staring at her yet again, looking at the changes time had wrought. There was a brittleness to her, a hardness that he was sure were new, not to mention a certain wariness. As if she viewed everything as a threat.

He recognised that wariness. He'd seen it in the eyes of people he'd worked for in his years of the black hat hacking that he'd done for the Russian mob. The wariness of people who have been hurt and now distrusted everyone they met.

Still, that was what happened when you grew up the way they had both grown up. You learned about the cruelty of the world, about the cruelty of people, and that was something no one could prepare you for. You just had to deal with it.

He definitely wasn't curious as to where the little girl he remembered had gone, not at all. He'd left her behind the day he'd escaped that house and Banks, and it was a good thing he'd left her behind. Not that he'd had any choice in the matter since Banks had given him an ultimatum—he could leave, but he couldn't take Zoe with him. She had to stay. And since he had no idea how he was going to take care of himself let alone a fifteen-year-old, he'd let Banks keep her.

Zoe opened her mouth as if to argue, then closed it with a snap. But the sparks of temper in her eyes didn't glitter any less. 'Not until I get my dress,' she said. 'Wouldn't want you to have arrogantly ordered one and then for it to go to waste.'

Archimedes gritted his teeth. He couldn't force her into this and he couldn't make it go any faster, not now she'd dug her heels in. Another thing he remembered about her. She was stubborn as a mule and twice as ornery, and now she was doing it just to spite him, he was certain of it.

'What would you like to do while we wait then?' he asked sarcastically, trying, and failing, to shove his annoyance away. 'Chat about house prices? The traffic? The weather?'

'Or we could talk about why you left,' she said, her jaw at a belligerent angle.

Fuck. That was the one conversation he didn't want to have. Because he suspected that she wasn't interested so much in why he'd left, but why he'd left without telling her, and he couldn't explain that with Banks standing right there.

'You still remember that?' he asked instead. 'It was years ago, Zoe.'

Her jaw was tight, the expression on her lovely face very, very fixed. It was clear to him that yes, she still remembered.

'Oh, I don't,' she said airily. 'I was only curious.'

He didn't think it was only curiosity, but he didn't argue. These few minutes with her would soon be over, and then they could both get on with living their own lives again, so what was the point in carrying on about things that had happened so long ago?

'I mean…' She put her hands in the pockets of her jeans. 'We could also talk about how you got all the money you needed to start your company.'

Yes, and that was another topic he didn't want to talk about, not with her. Not with anyone. He'd been very careful to erase ten years of his past, the years before Ares, erasing all the things he'd done and all the things he'd seen, all the things he'd once been a part of and never would be again.

He was never going to revisit them. Never.

'Or,' he said, 'you could talk about why you're still working for Banks when all you wanted was to get out.'

An expression he couldn't read flickered briefly over her face.

'Little thing called loyalty,' she said tartly. 'Something you wouldn't understand.'

Another dig at him leaving, no doubt. Well, he couldn't change that. He'd left because all he'd wanted was to escape Banks, escape being told what to do all the damn time, to have some agency in his own goddamned life, that was why. He'd been tired of being used. Tired of being manipulated and threatened. Tired of all his work going to benefit Banks while he himself got nothing.

He wasn't going to apologise for it, and if Zoe was still angry after fifteen years, then that was her issue to deal with, not his.

At that moment the door to the church opened again and one of his staff entered carrying a garment bag and a bouquet of flowers. Pink peonies, as ordered.

Archimedes strode over to the man and took both the garment bag and the flowers then turned and brandished them at Zoe.

'Your gown and flowers,' he said shortly. 'Get dressed and let's get this pointless ritual finished.'

'Very nice,' Banks said approvingly. 'What a kind gesture.'

Zoe meanwhile said nothing, her jaw tight. 'Thanks, but I've changed my mind,' she said. 'I'll stick to my jeans and T-shirt.'

Again, she was doing it to spite him, he had no doubt. If so, it was a mistake, especially with his patience already being so thin on the ground.

'Put the fucking gown on,' he ordered through gritted teeth. 'Because if you don't, I will invoice you for it and also for the flowers, and considering both were astronomically expensive, I'm sure you don't want me to do that.'

Zoe's silver gaze flamed, meeting his head-on, her strong, stubborn will pushing against his. But he didn't look away, because she wasn't the only one with a strong, stubborn will, and his had been honed through years of dealing with the worst and most dangerous of humanity. One small woman was nothing.

Except, for some reason, he could feel tension starting to gather between them, a very distinct tension. A familiar tension even. Her cheeks had become a little pink and he was suddenly aware that her bottom lip was very lush-looking and very soft. That the sparks in her eyes were hot, and that it might not be anger this time but something else, something more intense.

You should look away.

Yes, he should. Because if he held her gaze any longer it was going to turn into something it shouldn't. Yet...there was challenge in her eyes, as if she was goading him, needling him, wanting him to be the first to look away, and he could never do that. Backing down wasn't something he ever did.

'Please,' Banks murmured. 'We haven't got all day.'

Zoe's gaze flickered under the weight of his, and she glanced away. Muttering imprecations, she grabbed the garment bag and the flowers and strode off through a door near the altar, presumably to do what she was told.

Archimedes knew he shouldn't feel satisfied about

that, just as he shouldn't be aware of this familiar yet unwanted energy coursing through his veins. And it *was* unwanted. Zoe wasn't the little girl he remembered, but she was still the foster sister he'd once protected, and feeling any kind of sexual desire for her was wrong. Very wrong. Especially within the context of this ridiculous blackmail situation.

He couldn't think why he'd even felt it in the first place. Perhaps it was simply that he needed sex. He'd been working hard and hadn't put it into his schedule, which he normally did. Sometimes he preferred a spontaneous hookup, but mostly he organised it in advance with one of his semi-regular partners.

Filing away a reminder to call Celeste once this was done, he ignored the tension and the strange flick of desire, and turned back to the altar.

Banks was looking at him speculatively, which he did not like. Had the old man seen that moment? Probably. He was sharp as a tack and picked up on most things, so he could use them against people at a later date.

Archimedes stared back, raising an eyebrow in wordless enquiry.

Banks only smiled.

A couple of minutes later, Zoe came back through the doorway, the colour in her cheeks still high, the belligerent spark in her eyes still there. She'd ditched the jeans and the T-shirt and jacket for the gown he'd bought her, and despite her obvious fury at having to wear it, she looked… Beautiful. There was no other word for it.

The fabric hugged and highlighted the generous curves he'd spotted earlier, cupping her breasts, pulling tight around her waist and hips, before flaring out in a swirl of white silk. Her hair was in a ponytail, but he had a strange urge to pull it out of its elastic, let it fall in a long, soft fall of black to her waist.

Odd. He didn't usually get hung up on a woman's hair.

She came over to where he stood, temper fully on show, and presented her back to him. 'Do up my zip, please.' Despite the 'please' it was clear that it was an order.

Much to his own surprise, Archimedes found himself a little amused. She wasn't letting him get away with anything, was she? Even when he'd supposedly won with the dress, she wasn't conceding any ground at all.

However, it wasn't until he'd grabbed the tab of her zip that he realised she'd won in other ways too, because in order to pull the zip up, he had to stand close to her. And it made him suddenly aware of the expanse of bare, pale skin revealed by the unzipped gown. The subtle heat of her body. Her scent, which was sweet and at odds with her barbed tongue, a dichotomy that was… arousing. He found slowly doing her zip up arousing too, especially with his knuckles nearly brushing her skin as he did so. It made him very aware that she'd also ditched her bra since the gown was strapless.

Had she done this on purpose to unsettle him? It wouldn't be the first time a woman had played sexual games with him, and normally, he enjoyed them. But this was Zoe, and their relationship had always been strictly platonic, especially because she'd been three years younger than he was.

If she did it on purpose, it worked. You are unsettled.

He pushed the thought away, doing up the last bit of her zip before deliberately stepping away. She turned back to him and he noticed that the colour in her cheeks had deepened. Interesting. Apparently, that had unsettled her too.

Not that he was going to do a thing about it. They would get married and then they'd go about their lives as if nothing had changed. Perhaps he could even spend his 'wedding' night with Celeste, do something about this inconvenient desire. Yes, that was an excellent idea.

Zoe turned, her heart beating strangely fast for reasons she couldn't quite identify. She could still feel the warmth of Archimedes's hand almost brushing her bare skin as he'd zipped her up, and she didn't like the way it made her feel.

She hadn't liked that moment between them, when she'd stared belligerently at him as he'd told her that he'd invoice her for the dress if she didn't wear it. At first, she'd been too incensed to notice the tension in the air between them, and then, when she had noticed, it had shocked her. And it was galling that the shock had made her look away from him, because it felt as if she'd given him a surrender she hadn't meant to give.

She shouldn't have said anything about a dress. That had been a stupid move, because now she had to wear a wedding gown and carry a bouquet of admittedly quite pretty flowers, as if she were getting married for real. As if all of this meant something to her, which it didn't.

Still, since she hadn't wanted to pay for the dress or the flowers, she'd stomped into the small room to change into the gown. Then she'd been unreasonably enraged to find that it fitted her perfectly, because of course Archimedes had got the size right.

It had been irritating that she hadn't been able to do the zip up, and she'd felt very self-conscious as she'd come back into the church, because everyone had looked at her. That wouldn't have bothered her in itself, but the fact that she never wore dresses, and hadn't been able to see what she looked like in this one, made her uncomfortable.

Electing to ignore everyone, she'd gone over to Archimedes to do her zip up because he was the one who'd bought the stupid thing, so the least he could do was zip her up. But as soon as she'd felt him grab the tab of the zip she'd known she'd made a mistake.

Because it had brought her close to him, and made her conscious of his tall, broad presence behind her, towering over her. Of the heat of his body and the scent of his aftershave. Bergamot, she thought, and maybe black pepper and cedar. She loved scents, it was her one feminine indulgence, and the scent of him had set her on edge, because it really shouldn't be so delicious.

Now, her heartbeat was fast and her breathing a little short, and she was even more annoyed than when she'd first walked in, because he should not, absolutely not, have any effect on her whatsoever.

Yes, she'd once had a giant crush on him, but that had died the day he'd walked out without a word. Also, she'd been fifteen back then, and her crush had involved fantasies of kisses, nothing more. Physical desire hadn't factored into it, so why it was factoring now, she had no idea. But she resented the hell out of it.

Archimedes's blue gaze was steady, betraying nothing. Which meant the unsettledness was all on her side. Great.

'A thank you would be nice,' he said.

A hot retort immediately sprang to her lips, but she swallowed it back. Bickering with him would only prolong this situation and there was no way she wanted that. So she merely shrugged her shoulders and turned, making her way over to where Banks stood at the altar.

'Finally,' he said warmly, smiling at her. 'You look lovely.'

She didn't smile back, nor did she look as Archimedes moved over to the altar to stand beside her. She kept her gaze stonily forward, clutching her flowers as the priest began the ceremony.

It seemed to take forever till she was to say her vows, and she was surprised when Archimedes dug into his pocket and brought out a pair of rings. Then he took her hand in his and every single thought she had went straight out of her head.

His touch was warm, making a fine net of electricity settle over her body, and sending prickles of heat sparking all over her skin. It shocked her enough that she found herself looking up at him, meeting his gaze in surprise. Again, though, he remained expressionless as he slid the ring onto her finger. It was a plain gold band, nothing fancy, though there was another surprise in that he'd got one for himself too.

She put it on his finger in return, this time steadfastly avoiding his gaze as she let go of his long, blunt fingers. She didn't want to meet it, which felt too much like surrender for her comfort, but again, making a meal out of this situation purely because she was angry with him would be pointless.

The priest intoned the rest of the ceremony, pronouncing them husband and wife, and then that Archimedes may kiss his new bride.

Zoe didn't expect that he would, so it came as yet another huge shock when those long fingers suddenly gripped her chin, tipping her face up, and his mouth brushed hers in the most featherlight and fleeting of kisses.

She froze. It was as if someone had hit her over the back of the head with something heavy, making her dizzy and her thought processes sluggish.

All she could think was that Archimedes had kissed her. He had *kissed* her. And the worst part of it was that even though it had been briefest of kisses, she could somehow feel it *everywhere*.

There was a heat clenching tight inside her, a part of herself she'd never paid much attention to. She'd been kissed before, of course, and there had been a few boyfriends. Not very many, but she'd had them, though she'd never slept with any of them. Sex had seemed like a huge step, a surrendering of trust to someone, and she had never felt as if she could trust anyone enough for that. The kisses she'd had had been pleasant and the touches okay, but nothing to write home about. Nothing that had made her want to take off her clothes for anyone.

But the light brush of Archimedes's mouth was a shock to the system, Sleeping Beauty being jolted awake, and then it was gone. He'd turned around to talk to Banks as if nothing had happened.

As if he hadn't just turned her world on its head.

Zoe pulled herself together and shoved her unwanted response as far away as it was possible to get. If nothing had happened for him, then nothing had happened for her either. But at least it was done now. She could get out of this ridiculous dress, give the flowers to a random stranger who might appreciate it, then get back to work.

The last formality was signing the documents and once that was done, Banks said, beaming, 'So, do you have any idea as to where you'll be living?'

Zoe opened her mouth to say that naturally they'd be staying in London, but again, Archimedes got in first.

'I have a villa on an island in the Cyclades. We'll be living there.'

Yet another shock went through her and she looked sharply at him. 'What do you mean "we"?'

Archimedes turned his expressionless blue gaze on her. 'One of the stipulations of this situation is that we live together, Zoe. Or did you miss that part of the agreement?'

'He's not wrong,' Banks said mildly. 'That is part of the deal.'

'Why?' Zoe looked at her foster father. 'What purpose can there possibly be for us to live together?'

Banks spread his hands. 'I want you two to mend fences,' he said. 'Archie left somewhat precipitously and I don't think you ever got over it.'

Zoe could feel her face get hot. 'Well, that's a lie,' she said, bitterly conscious that Archimedes had turned his attention to her as well.

'You didn't leave your room for a week, dear girl,' Banks said, blithely revealing her secrets to her hated enemy as if they were nothing. 'It affected your work, it affected everything. Also, how is this child to be conceived if you're not living together?'

The word 'conceive' made her face get even hotter, but Archimedes only said, 'We'll be living in Greece and that is final.'

The flat, certain way he said it incensed her. 'Are you completely insane?' she demanded, turning on him. 'Why the hell do I have to uproot myself and go to Greece? Why can't you stay in London?'

'What?' His brows drew down, making him look even more demonic. 'You mean stay with you in whatever cramped little flat you're living in? I think not.'

Zoe stared, momentarily speechless. He stared back, his blue gaze utterly impenetrable. There was no give in that gaze. No mercy either, and a thought floated through her head. What had happened to him to make him so hard? So unyielding? She didn't remember him being like that. No, with her, he'd always been kind and patient and protective, yet there was no sign of that boy in the man that stood in front of her now.

'You can't just decide for me.' She tried to sound reasonable instead of squawking like a fishwife. 'We need to discuss this first.'

'No,' he said. 'I've already decided. You can do your work remotely, so it really doesn't matter where you live, does it?'

'But I have friends and—'

'Do you, Zoe?' he interrupted, his gaze settling on her, hard and sharp and edged. 'Or are you just being bloody-minded?'

'How dare you? I'm—'

'You wanted to leave London behind you, that's what you used to tell me. You couldn't wait to leave, to go somewhere else. Well, you can come and live with me in Greece. It's only for a year and then you can come back here if you're that miserable.'

Zoe wanted very much to punch his stupid, handsome face. Because he wasn't wrong. All she'd wanted when she was a kid was to get away, see the world, spend some time elsewhere that wasn't dark, grey, dreary London. And the fact that not only did he remember that she'd said it but was also using it against her rubbed like steel wool against exposed nerves.

'Isn't marriage supposed to be a partnership?' she asked, trying to mask her outrage.

'This isn't a real marriage,' he said. 'Also, I'm not arguing about this. I have meetings this afternoon and I need to be in Athens by tomorrow. We'll leave tonight.'

Banks was also frowning. 'I didn't think that Greece would be—'

'Greece is my homeland.' Archimedes turned his

razor-sharp gaze on his foster father instead. 'You wanted us to live together and so we will. But not in London. End of story.'

Zoe wanted to keep arguing, though it was strange to have Banks on her side for a change, because she didn't think arguing to stay in London was too much to ask. 'You can't make me,' she said.

Archimedes glanced at her. 'I can,' he said with the air of a man who got whatever he wanted, whenever he wanted it. 'But I suggest that you agree because you won't want that, I assure you.'

Yes, he was harder. Meaner. He used to care about her feelings. He used to care about her, but it looked as if all those feelings were dead and gone.

So why turn this into an issue?

True. Because it didn't need to be. The truth was that she *did* want to get out of London and the thought of living for the next year on an island in Greece wasn't… unattractive. She could absolutely work remotely, and perhaps if it hadn't been Archimedes who'd suggested it, or even if he'd asked her first, she would have happily agreed.

But he'd ordered her to do it, no doubt assuming she'd fall into line without protest, the way she used to whenever he suggested anything. And it felt dangerous not to at least put up some kind of cursory argument. The boy he'd once been was one thing, but the man he was now was another thing entirely. A stranger. A hard, cold, imperious stranger.

Still, arguing about it betrayed strong feelings, and she didn't have strong feelings about him, not any more.

If he wanted to drag her all the way to Greece, he was welcome to drag her. But once they got there, if he was expecting her to acquiesce to whatever he wanted, he was going to be disappointed.

'Fine,' she said, trying to say it with less ill grace than she actually felt. 'Greece it is.'

CHAPTER THREE

ARCHIMEDES STARED AT his new wife, sitting in the seat opposite him. They were in his jet, on their way to the private Cycladic island he'd bought a couple of years earlier when he'd been investigating his parents. Or rather, his father.

His mother, who'd walked away when he was five, he'd decided not to bother with since she'd made it so clear that she wanted nothing to do with him. But his father, he did want to know about. While Archimedes had been working for the Russians, he'd had some contacts track Julius Athineos down. He'd eventually been located in an Athens prison doing time for murder, so that had been that. Archimedes hadn't even bothered with a visit.

He'd then decided he was his own person and had nothing to do with the two people who'd made him, and as such, he'd make his own home for himself in his country of origin. So when a beautiful jewel of an island had come up for sale, he'd bought it. He never spent much time on Kythea since he never spent much time in any one place, but he liked that he had it.

Zoe hadn't appreciated him ordering her to go there

with him, though. In retrospect, he supposed he could have worded it better, but her insistence on staying in London had been ridiculous. All she'd wanted was to get out of London and away from Banks—at least when she was a kid that was all she'd wanted, in addition to her travel dreams. Perhaps things were different now she was adult. Whatever, the last thing he'd wanted was to stand around arguing about where they were going to live, and so he'd made a decision. Not in London, with Banks constantly looking in, but on an island away from Banks entirely. If she ended up not liking it, well, she could go back to London and he wouldn't argue. But if she did, well. She'd end up thanking him, he was sure of it.

She was sitting cross-legged in the seat, her attention fixed on her laptop screen. He'd gone to her flat—and he'd been right, it *was* cramped—to find that the only bag she was bringing was a duffel bag full of clothes and her laptop. That was it. He hadn't questioned it, privately thinking that if she needed anything he could always get it for her.

On the trip to the airport and now, in the plane, she kept her attention firmly on her laptop, not bothering to say more than a couple of words to him.

He was surprised to find that it annoyed him. Not that he was a fan of small talk, but it would have been nice if she'd at least greeted him. They weren't complete strangers, after all. They were actually married.

It was a strange thought, her being his wife. It had been strange standing at the altar with her, no matter how many times he told himself that it meant nothing.

Strange to put the ring he'd bought—because rings were part of the wedding ceremony—on her finger. The ring meant nothing, too. Just as the vows he'd made meant nothing. They were empty. They weren't going to love or cherish each other till death did them part, or look after each other in sickness and in health. And they definitely weren't going to be forsaking all others. Though, kissing her had been a mistake.

He'd known she was expecting him *not* to, so naturally he'd decided that he would. She'd been needling him since the moment she'd walked into the church, and he wasn't above getting a little of his own back. When he'd turned her face up and bent to brush his mouth over hers he'd expected to feel absolutely nothing. But that hadn't happened. Instead, he'd been abruptly and forcefully made aware of how soft her lips were and how warm they felt beneath his. How he'd wanted to deepen the kiss just to see what she tasted like.

A stupid move. He wouldn't make that mistake again. When they got to Kythea, he'd call Celeste, get her to join him for the evening. Perhaps he'd even fly her out to the island. Zoe wouldn't care.

'Stop looking at me,' Zoe said without looking up. 'You're distracting me.'

He shifted in his seat, annoyed by how aware he was of one long, black lock of hair that had fallen forward over her shoulder and was now curling around the curve of one breast.

'Then stop being distracting,' he said.

'I'm doing nothing but sitting here.'

Archimedes shifted again. He hated flying, and not

because it made him nervous. He hated being constrained in a long metal tube with nothing to do but sit. Normally, he'd be walking up and down in the aisle making phone calls, yet for some reason he'd found himself studying Zoe instead.

'Why did you say yes?' he asked, curious.

'Say yes to what?' Her gaze remained on her laptop screen.

'Yes to coming to Kythea.'

'I mean, you didn't give me much of a choice.'

'I gave you a choice. You didn't have to come.'

'Banks wanted us to live together so if you were going to be in Greece I also had to come to Greece. Anyway, I decided it didn't matter to me that much.'

He studied her face, noting the lines of concentration on her forehead. When she'd been young, she'd used to bite her tongue in concentration and he'd used to tease her about it. He glanced down at her mouth, the lips he'd kissed just a few hours earlier, and sure enough, she was biting her tongue. The sight made a strange warmth settle somewhere behind his breastbone, even as it made other parts of him tighten in reaction.

He ignored those parts of him.

'Then why did you argue?' he asked, because he thought that wasn't true. She actually *did* mind quite a bit, but didn't want him knowing that.

'Because you were being a complete dick.'

He decided to let that go since he couldn't argue with it. He had been a dick. Then again, he wasn't exactly known for his winning way with people. After leaving Banks's house, he'd developed into a shark—he'd had to, dealing with the Russians—and had remained one. Anyway, he was impatient and was tired of bickering with her.

'What is Banks offering you?' he asked instead. 'To buy into this stupid scheme of his.'

'None of your business.' She started typing very fast, the keys making soft clicking noises. The sound of his childhood.

'So is that how we're going to do things?' he asked, not sure why he was pushing this. Perhaps because he had nothing better to do. 'We're not even going to talk?'

'I don't want to talk,' she said calmly. 'What I want is to do my work and be left alone.'

'And the child?'

This time her attention wavered and finally, she glanced over the top of her screen at him, a bright flash of silver. 'What about it?' Her tone was flat and unfriendly.

'Well, we're going to have to conceive a child somehow over the course of this year.'

Her gaze flickered and he found himself going very still. Had her thoughts gone to the bedroom at the mention of conception? Was that what she was thinking? There had been that moment in the church, after all, when they'd stared at each other and he'd known that she'd felt the tension between them wind tight. And then there had been that instance when he'd taken her fingers in his to slide her ring on, and she'd looked up at him, her grey eyes wide. Also, that kiss, and he'd felt her go very, very still…

But no, he wasn't going to think about any of that.

Whatever the jolt that went through him the moment his mouth brushed hers had meant, it wasn't something he'd pursue. Even if he'd been sure he saw her eyes darken in response.

'Parthenogenesis,' she said without missing a beat.

Amusement curled through him for the second time in twenty-four hours, which was unheard of.

'Ah,' he said. 'Sadly, that only happens with plants and some invertebrates, not human beings. You will need a donation from me.'

'If you want to sleep with me,' she said, returning her gaze to the laptop, 'the answer is no.'

'Sleeping with you was the last thing on my mind,' he replied, both to her and to a thin thread of desire that was slowly winding through him, no matter how many times he ignored it. 'I'll be engaging a fertility doctor.'

'There we are then. Problem solved.'

'That will involve us meeting.' He didn't know why he was insisting on talking about this.

'No, it won't,' she disagreed. 'You make your "donation" in one room, I'll do whatever I need to do in another. We won't have to see each other at all.'

Archimedes shifted yet again, annoyed for reasons he couldn't explain. She was being very calm and measured, not at all the little spitfire she'd been in the church, and it made him restless. It made him want to keep needling her, keep pushing her until he made her grey eyes spark again.

'What if I insist we have dinner together?' he said. 'Every evening.'

'No, thank you.'

That made him even more restless and now irritated into the bargain. Both with himself for pushing and with her for not even looking at him while they were having this discussion. So he leaned forward, reached out and pushed her laptop closed.

Her head jerked up, and yes, there it was, the outrage glittering in her eyes. 'What the hell are you doing?'

He held her gaze. 'Dinner. With me. Every night.'

She didn't look away. 'Why?'

'Because I said so.' Again, he couldn't really articulate his reasons for demanding they have dinner together every night, apart from a childish, bloody-minded reaction to her refusal to even look at him. Whatever, now he'd said it, and now she'd denied him, he was going to insist.

'In that case, definitely not.'

Archimedes gritted his teeth. 'Put it this way, would you prefer to come of your own free will, or be escorted to the dinner table by one of my security guards?'

Zoe scowled. 'What are you going to do? March me there at gunpoint?'

His irritation deepened. He'd walked himself into a trap, which was incredibly short-sighted, not to mention very unlike him. Because of course he didn't want to march her there at gunpoint. He could, if necessary, but...was it really necessary? He was a man who got what he wanted when he wanted it and did not like being denied. Most of the time everyone fell in with his wishes because he was simply too powerful, too rich and too dangerous not to.

Zoe, however, was not everyone. She was his one-time foster sister and she had no fear of him—there was certainly only annoyance in her silver eyes right now, for example—and so he was in the uncomfortable and unfamiliar situation of having to use a hammer to crack an egg.

Still, he was the one who'd brought up his security and he couldn't back down, not without giving in to her, and he couldn't do that.

'If necessary,' he said curtly.

Zoe's stare became as sharp as a needle. 'Is that how we're going to do this? If I say no you're going to use security to force me? Good thing we're not conceiving this baby the old-fashioned way.'

The words shouldn't have had any effect on him at all, and yet the moment she said them, a vision popped into his mind, of her in his bed, her black hair spread over the white cotton of his sheets, her eyes dark with desire.

Naturally, as soon as he imagined that, her gaze flickered again, almost the same flicker that he'd seen just a moment before when he'd said the word 'conceive'.

That thin thread of desire tightened abruptly and he could tell that she, too, was aware of what she'd just said and was also thinking about it, because her cheeks had become even more flushed.

'Who's to say we can't?' he said, very, very unwisely.

Her flush deepened into red and she reached forward and pushed his hand very decisively off her laptop. 'Not in a million years,' she snapped. 'Now, for God's sake, let me bloody work.'

Hacking computers was all about finding a weakness and exploiting it, and he'd spent too many years doing just that not to know a weakness when he saw one. And he was looking at one right now.

She was blushing and if he wasn't much mistaken, the pulse at the base of her throat, just above the neckline of her T-shirt, was racing. He knew what attraction looked like in a woman and attraction was written all over her lovely face.

Interesting. He hadn't anticipated that would factor anywhere in this little scenario, and back in the church he'd been vaguely horrified at himself for feeling it for her. But…perhaps it would come in handy at some point.

'Dinner,' he said, sitting back in his seat. 'Tonight. We can discuss it.'

Zoe's heart was beating uncomfortably fast, her cheeks burning. It was galling. All he'd done was lean forward and push her laptop closed. He wasn't even that near and yet…the look in his blue eyes had made her mouth go dry.

She didn't understand what was happening to her and she didn't like it one bit. Just as she didn't like *anything* to do with Archimedes Athineos. Her new husband.

She still couldn't believe she was on a plane heading to Greece, let alone being married to her erstwhile foster brother, yet here she was doing exactly those things.

Deciding early on that she wasn't going to speak to him if she didn't need to, she'd packed the minimum amount possible—she didn't need much anyway—and as soon as he'd picked her up that evening, she'd opened her laptop and had proceeded to ignore him, though it hadn't been easy.

She'd been uncomfortably aware of him sitting next to her in the car, the heat of his thigh right next to hers, that delicious scent of his filling the confined space. She'd been glad once they'd transferred onto the plane, so she wouldn't have to sit next to him. But then he'd commandeered the seat opposite her, again with his long legs out in front of him, taking up as much space as humanly possible.

She might have been able to ignore that if he hadn't spent the past half an hour staring at her. She'd attempted to ignore that as well, but his stare had a weight to it, a pressure that was incredibly distracting.

Even as a kid she remembered him having a kind of tense, kinetic energy. He could never sit still unless he was at the computer screen. He always had to be doing something. Even now, even with that energy contained, she could still feel it steadily burning, bright and hot as a flame.

She hadn't wanted to say anything to him, or even acknowledge that she was aware of his stare, but in the end she'd had to say something. He was too distracting and she didn't like how it made her feel antsy and restless herself.

She hadn't expected him to ask her why she'd changed her mind, though, or that he'd insist on having dinner with her, for reasons she couldn't begin to imagine. She was still furious with him for insisting they live in Greece without even asking her, and now he was insisting on dinner, again without asking her. Especially when his reasons for wanting dinner were 'because he said so'.

His peremptorily shutting her laptop had been egregious, as was the mention of a 'security guard' escorting her to this stupid dinner, and she'd unfortunately let her temper get the better of her and made that dig about conception. And as soon as the words were out of her mouth, she wished she hadn't said them.

Because she'd seen a spark in his blue eyes, a hot spark, and felt the small flame that had flickered into life when he'd kissed her leap higher in response. And she didn't want it to. She didn't want to see that spark in his eyes either, because her being attracted to him was one thing, but knowing that attraction was reciprocated was quite another.

She didn't want to get into anything physical with him. In fact, he was the last man she'd ever sleep with, because again, there was that trust issue and she didn't trust him as far as she could throw him. She'd spent too long being furious with him, and physical attraction was too complicated to deal with right now, especially when they were going to be spending a year living in the same house together.

Yet telling herself all of that made no difference to the race of her heart, or the way her skin had tightened. Or how painfully conscious of him sitting opposite she was, with his long powerful legs stretched arrogantly out in front of him, his intense blue gaze on her as if the rest of the world didn't exist.

No one had looked at her like that for a very long time, if they ever had.

'Well?' he said impatiently.

'Is that a request?' she shot back. 'Because it didn't sound like one, in which case you don't need a response, do you?' She was half inclined to refuse again, just to see if he'd make good on his threat to have a security guard drag her to the dinner table. After all, why not make this as difficult for him as possible?

He shifted in his seat, frowning. 'It's just dinner, Zoe, not an interrogation.'

'Really? Well, you mentioned having a security guard escorting me to the dinner table so, as you can see, I'm a little confused as to what you're actually asking for.'

He let out a breath as if frustrated. 'I want to talk to you. It's been fifteen years, and I'd like to know how you're doing.'

Well, that was better than 'because I said so'.

'You really want to know?'

'Yes.' There was no hesitation in his voice. 'Is that so wrong?'

'No, of course it isn't. But it does beg the question as to why you waited fifteen years to "see how I was doing".'

His hard mouth tightened, blue eyes glinting. 'I got caught up in work. Life got in the way, et cetera, et cetera.'

'I see.' She heard the lie in his voice and didn't quite know whether to call him on it.

'Why?' he asked. 'Did you miss me?'

'No, of course not,' she said stoutly. 'I never thought of you.'

He stared at her in silence for a moment, his gaze sharp, and she could feel herself beginning to blush yet again. Especially when one corner of his mouth lifted.

'So you did miss me,' he said, a satisfied note in his voice.

She didn't want to look away, didn't want to give him any kind of surrender, and yet she couldn't hold his gaze any longer, so she glanced down at her laptop, opening the screen again. 'If you want me at dinner, you can send a security guard,' she said. 'I'm not coming otherwise.'

She didn't need to look at him to feel his annoyance. It radiated from him like a fire radiating heat, and that made her feel unreasonably satisfied.

Weren't you not *going to keep bickering with him?*

That was the idea. But he was being such a dick she couldn't help herself.

'If you're going to put me to the trouble of getting a security guard to escort you, then I'm going to put you to the trouble of dressing for the occasion,' he said at last.

Zoe went still, then jerked her head up to meet his steady gaze. 'Dress? What do you mean dress?'

'It'll be our wedding dinner.' Challenge glinted in his eyes. 'So I think we should dress accordingly.'

Immediately, she wanted to tell him to go to hell,

but she could see he was expecting her to say that. So of course she had to do the opposite. It went against her every instinct but she gave him a saccharine smile instead.

'I'd love to dress up. But unfortunately, I didn't bring a nice dress.'

'That won't be a problem,' he said with the same calm. 'I'm sure I can find you something appropriate.'

'You have a lot of women's dresses in your wonderful Greek villa then?'

'I do,' he agreed. 'I do quite a bit of entertaining there.'

'Entertaining your thousands of mistresses?'

Again, that irritatingly sexy half smile curled one corner of his mouth.

'How do you know that I have thousands of mistresses?'

A little jolt went through her, and she cursed herself silently. She hadn't been able to help reading about him in various business publications and online gossip columns. And while his mistresses might not number in the thousands, they definitely numbered in the hundreds, she was sure. He did have somewhat of a playboy reputation.

'It was an assumption,' she said, trying to cover her mistake. 'Billionaires aren't generally known for their commitment to celibacy.'

He laughed and something shivered through her, because that laugh was as sexy as that smile. In fact, it was downright illegally so. She didn't like, either, that a small part of her was pleased with herself for getting one out of him. She'd used to love hearing him laugh. He'd never been free with them but she'd always managed to get one out of him, and the sound had never failed to make her happy too.

'That's true,' he admitted. 'But rest assured, my list of conquests is not in the thousands.'

'What a relief,' she said sarcastically. 'You had me worried there for a minute.'

'Why?' One lazy brow rose. 'Thinking of adding yourself to the list?'

Right on cue, she could again feel the blush spread over her cheeks. Not for the first time, she wished she wasn't quite so pale.

'I'd rather die,' she said, unable to keep the edge from her voice.

'I'm sure you wouldn't.' He was still smiling, no doubt satisfied that he'd got a rise out of her. 'There are worse things than being in my bed.'

Zoe fiercely wished he would stop saying words like 'bed' and 'mistresses'. She wished her own brain wouldn't immediately take the word 'bed' and run with it, thinking about what it would be like to be one of his mistresses, to be in his bed.

'Do you mind?' She glanced down at her laptop screen once more. 'I'm trying to work.'

'You were the one who mentioned conception and mistresses, not me.'

Zoe gritted her teeth and ignored him.

'I have some gowns for you to choose from,' he went on. 'I'll have my housekeeper lay out a selection for you.'

Of course, he had a housekeeper. He wasn't the poor orphan she'd come to know and love in Banks's house. The driven, distractible boy who had nothing, like all the others in that house, but it didn't matter because they were all in it together.

No, he was a big deal now. He owned Ares Security, whose online security systems were supposedly impregnable, and he was worth billions of dollars. She'd read that he had houses everywhere and never stayed in the same place more than a week. Which was the only thing that made the thought of living in Greece supportable. He'd only be there a week and then he'd be gone.

She'd been a bit worried about leaving Banks on his own, but Banks had insisted he'd be fine, that she shouldn't be concerned about him. So maybe instead of worrying, she should do something really useful while she was there. Maybe she could work on hacking Ares' security systems, just for fun. There was always a weakness, always a back door, and she, like Archimedes, was very, very good at finding it, even if the system was supposedly 'impregnable'. That would wipe that smug smile off his face.

After all, the Titanic was supposed to be 'unsinkable'.

'I'll find some jewellery for you,' Archimedes went on, clearly warming to his theme. 'Also, lipstick if you please. Shoes too.'

He was goading her now, and she shouldn't rise to the bait, she really shouldn't.

'How about you stick that jewellery, lipstick and

shoes up your arse?' she snapped back, unable to help herself.

Archimedes only laughed again. 'This is going to be a *very* interesting dinner.'

CHAPTER FOUR

THE JET CAME in to land on Kythea's tiny landing strip and from there Archimedes had a small Jeep take them to his villa. It was built on the side of a rocky cliff high above the sea, with traditional whitewashed thick stone walls, many terraces, small gardens, olive groves and grapevines. Some of his staff did small batch olive oil pressing, which they then sold to tourists on the mainland. He didn't bother charging them rent for the trees or the buildings that they used to press the olives because he loved the oil that they made. He also loved that they gave it to him free in return for use of the groves and the buildings.

Zoe kept her attention firmly on the scenery, her face betraying nothing as they drove up the narrow, winding road to the villa itself. Cypress trees stood on either side of the entrance, artfully lit in the summer night that was already closing in.

There was a brief kerfuffle when one of his staff tried to take Zoe's bag to her room and she protested, but after he'd told her that she was welcome to lug the heavy bag up the stairs to her room herself, she eventually relented. He did insist on showing her to her room, though, because he'd given the order to Lydia, his housekeeper, to find a selection of gowns for his new wife and he wanted to see her reaction.

Yes, he was a bastard, he could fully admit that. He hadn't needed to insist on dinner, and he certainly hadn't needed to rub it in by insisting on gowns, lipstick, jewellery and shoes either, but she was being so bloody-minded he hadn't been able to resist.

Also, he was beginning to enjoy himself and that was quite unexpected. In fact, he couldn't remember the last time he'd enjoyed himself so much in the company of another person that wasn't directly related to sex. Or the intellectual enjoyment of successfully hacking someone's security, or building systems that kept hackers out.

But then Zoe had always been quick-witted, he remembered that. She'd been such a bright spark back in Banks's house. He remembered the first night she'd arrived, small and bedraggled-looking, with huge grey eyes. Banks had introduced her to the rest of them—there had been five at that stage, with Zoe making it six. She had been afraid, flinching as one of the bigger boys nearly knocked into her, and almost without thinking about it, he'd pushed the other boy away to protect her.

Back then, he'd been a chaotic mess of a kid, his impulse control nonexistent, and his morals skewed by his environment. He hadn't made friends with any of the other kids, mainly because he just hadn't been interested in them.

Then along had come Zoe, and her vulnerability had

hooked into a deep part of himself he hadn't known was there. Why her? He had no idea. Perhaps she'd reminded him of himself when he'd first arrived in Banks's house, alone and scared, coming from yet another foster situation that hadn't worked out.

Whatever the reason, when he'd pushed that other boy away, she'd looked at him as if he was her own personal hero. No one had ever looked at him that way before, and he'd liked it. He'd wanted more of it.

So he'd become her protector and gradually she'd come out of her shell. The first time she'd smiled at him, he felt he'd won a prize, and the first time she'd put her small hand in his, his heart had swelled in his chest. She'd been the first bright spark in his dark, lonely world. The first person who'd ever wanted to spend time with him, the first person who'd ever shown interest in him that wasn't just about his ability with a keyboard.

He'd loved that. Loved that she trusted him and looked up to him. It had made him feel as if there was something better inside him, something more than just a mess of a kid who nobody had wanted.

Then he'd discovered she was fiercely intelligent into the bargain, and after the requisite Banks lessons in computer hacking she was also nearly as proficient as he was when it came to moving around in the data sphere. That hadn't made him jealous. That had made him fiercely proud.

Now, as he led her up the stairs to where her room was, he could feel an echo of that pride inside him. The ghost of a feeling he'd long since thought was gone. A feeling he never had any more, not these days.

A feeling you should never allow yourself to feel.

No, there was that. There were many things he no longer allowed himself to feel, because he knew what happened if he followed those feelings. Darkness. Violence. Death. A hole he'd spent years climbing out of.

But he wasn't going to descend into that hole again, not now he'd successfully mastered all the emotions associated with it, and he never would.

He led her down the hallway to the guest room in one corner of the villa that had a balcony and a magnificent view out over the ocean. It was a beautiful room, light and airy, with a huge bed hung with gauzy curtains, a colourfully tiled ensuite bathroom, a daybed near the windows and a massive walk-in wardrobe. The floor was smooth stone flags softened with bright rugs, and cushions that echoed the colours of the rugs were scattered on the bed and the daybed.

He gestured to her to go in and she walked past him into the room. Right in front of her was the bed with the four gowns laid carefully out on it, that Lydia had chosen according to his specifications.

One was green silk, another silver net with a black underdress. There was a slinky little black dress, and the last was scarlet silk with a hip-high slit in the skirt. She would look magnificent in any of them, and he was rather pleased with himself for insisting she wear them.

Zoe dumped her duffel bag, then walked up to the bed and looked down at the array of gowns. She glanced at him, her silver gaze unimpressed.

'How many other women have worn these?' she asked bluntly.

'Why?' he asked, purely for wickedness' sake. 'Are you jealous?'

She snorted. 'Hell, no. I just don't like second-hand clothes.'

That was a lie. She'd worn nothing but second-hand clothes as a kid and had never had any problem with them. No, it wasn't the clothes she didn't like, it was doing what he said, wasn't it?

'No other women have worn these gowns,' he said with perfect truth. 'They're brand-new.'

'Okay, so you just happened to have a whole lot of gowns in your wardrobe for…what? Emergencies?'

'Something like that.' He strolled over to the bed and stood beside her. 'I think the silver would look amazing on you.' Nothing wrong with a little reverse psychology, especially when what he really wanted was for her to wear the slinky black dress. In fact, it surprised him how much he wanted her to wear it. Seeing her in that wedding gown had whetted his appetite, and even though he shouldn't feed that appetite, looking wouldn't hurt.

'Don't tell me,' she said tartly. 'You're going to insist on that silver one.'

'No.' He lifted a shoulder. 'You can choose which one you'd like.'

'Oh, wow, how generous of you.' Sarcasm edged the words. 'Finally, I can make a choice of my own.'

He didn't rise to the bait, merely giving her a bland look. 'The shoes are in the wardrobe, along with the jewellery. The lipstick is in the bathroom, along with other make-up.'

She didn't look at him, but he could tell by the way her jaw was jutting that she was battling her temper. He was standing right next to her and he could smell her delicious feminine scent, complex, sweet, yet also warm, with an undertone of spice. It was sexy as hell.

'Believe it or not,' he said conversationally, 'dinner and dressing up for it are the only things I'm going to insist on. As to anything else, I don't care.'

'Your generosity knows no bounds.' Her nose wrinkled as she surveyed the gowns on offer. Then she glanced at him. 'I'm not the only one dressing up. If you're not, then it's a hefty no thank you from me.'

'Of course.' He gave her a smile purely to annoy her. 'It wouldn't be right to let you have all the spotlight.' He nodded at his feet then held up his hand with his new wedding ring on his finger. 'I have the shoes and jewellery on already.'

'But no lipstick, I see,' she said.

Again, she managed to get a genuine smile from him. 'No. No lipstick for me.'

'I should make you.'

'With your own security guard?'

This time she rolled her eyes before looking back down at the gowns on the bed. 'What if I don't like any of these?'

'Then please feel free to turn up naked,' he murmured, again unable to help himself. 'I wouldn't object.'

Her gaze narrowed, but she couldn't quite hide the

faint pink in her cheeks. He was becoming addicted to that blush of hers, which wasn't good in the bigger scheme of things. Being addicted to anything wasn't good in the bigger scheme of things, as he well knew.

He'd left Banks's house determined to never be under anyone's control ever again—he'd wanted to be his own man, his own master—but he'd always planned to take Zoe with him. When Banks had refused to let her go, he'd felt it like a knife in his side. So he'd decided then and there that he would *make* Banks let her go, pry her from his grip. At eighteen, though, he'd had nothing, he *was* nothing, which meant that he had become someone. Someone so powerful and important and rich that Banks would have no choice but to give her to him.

There were no high-earning jobs for an eighteen-year-old with no formal schooling, so he'd turned to the criminal underworld instead. He'd managed to get an in with a Russian gang who'd needed someone with hacking skills and no morals. The work was exciting and, best of all, well-paid, and so he'd taken the job without a second thought. That had led to more jobs, more excitement, more money. He hadn't cared what the job was about. He hadn't cared that what he was doing was illegal. All that mattered was earning money so that he could get back to Zoe.

But then the gang had started to feel like family to him. They'd treated him as if he were one of their own, and that had given him power. That had given him status. He'd loved the feeling of being the one in control, and he'd pursued it relentlessly. He forgot about Zoe. He became one of them, dealing out violence when necessary, destroying lives without a single shred of regret, everything good in him consumed by the adrenaline rush of power. He had become a monster.

But then, ten years later, his road-to-Damascus moment happened.

Some contacts in Athens that he'd had search for his father finally sent him their findings, and it had pinged in his inbox one morning after a bender on Niklaus's yacht.

He'd lain there in bed with a hangover of monstrous proportions, two women sleeping beside him, reading the file on his phone, conscious of how every single forgotten dream he'd had as a little boy, of his father being a hero and coming to rescue him, had never been going to happen.

His father was nothing but a brutal thug who'd ended up in prison after murdering someone in a street fight. That was when Archimedes had sat up and looked around him, at the evidence of his own excess, thought about the last ten years of his life, and he'd realised something.

He was just the same. He might not be in prison, he might have more money than he knew what to do with, but he was the same brutal thug his father was.

Joining the Russians was supposed to have made him rich and powerful. He was supposed to be someone, and yet all he'd become was a monster. And even worse than that, he was in a darker, more violent family than he had been at Banks's house. Nothing had changed.

Archimedes had left Banks so he could be in control of his own life, and yet here he was, in the darkness again, in control of nothing, a slave to his own appetites and desires. That couldn't continue. He wouldn't allow it. He wasn't going to be his father, and he wasn't going to be another Banks. He was going to be different, and this time he would control his appetites. They would never again control him.

So he'd left the gang, used his money to start Ares, and this time he stayed on the right side of the law.

Sex had been one of the things he'd indulged in shamelessly in the past, but now he was much more careful when it came to managing his physical desires. He allowed himself a night with a woman once a week, but that woman would never be Zoe, he'd already decided that.

You shouldn't use sex against her then.

No, he shouldn't. Given that she'd blushed at the mildest of innuendos, she probably wasn't as experienced as he was, which made it unfair of him to use those tactics on her.

Strange to think that he actually cared about fairness or otherwise, because normally he didn't. Zoe had always been the one with a strong sense of fairness and justice, not him. In fact, normally, he didn't care much about anything at all except his company, still less someone else's feelings. Then again, she wasn't merely 'someone else'. She was Zoe. His foster sister.

The thought made a thread of irritation wrap around him, and he said, without thinking about it, 'I'm going to have Celeste visit me tonight.'

She frowned. 'Celeste?'

'A lover of mine. It is my wedding night, after all, and it's not a wedding night without sex.'

Zoe blinked as if she didn't understand what he was saying. 'You mean you're going to fly in a lover of yours on our wedding night so you can have sex?'

'Yes. I didn't think you'd object.' He found himself studying her, though what he was looking for he didn't quite know. 'Unless you do?'

Her gaze flickered, and she looked back down at the bed again. 'Oh, no,' she said. 'Fly in your lover. Hell, fly in three or four, I don't care.'

Did she, though? Did she care? More to the point, did he? Normally, he wouldn't even have mentioned flying a lover in, he would have just done it and if people didn't like it, they could go to hell. Yet, far from not caring what she thought, he was irritated still further at her apparent acceptance.

You used to care what she thought.

Yes, but that had been a long time ago, when he'd been a kid. And that kid was gone, crushed in the web of excess and violence that had ensnared him after he'd left Banks.

He'd never be that kid again, and now he'd walked himself into a trap. How extremely annoying. He really *had* to fly Celeste in now, because if he didn't, Zoe would no doubt wonder why, and perhaps make connections he didn't want her to make.

'Good,' he said. 'She'll probably come in quite late.'

'That's fine,' Zoe said. 'And, speaking of lovers, I'm

assuming you'll be fine with me shipping in whichever guy I want to sleep with, too.'

A curious emotion went through him then, something strong and angry and quite unfamiliar. He'd never been a possessive man—to be possessive, you had to care about something—but there was no doubting the possessiveness in him now.

It shouldn't matter if she wanted to ship in a lover. He shouldn't care. He had no feelings about her either way, except maybe a vague physical attraction and maybe a ghost of that old protectiveness he'd once felt years ago. That was all.

'Perfectly fine,' he managed to force out in as casual a tone as he could muster. 'We could all have dinner together.'

Zoe pulled a face. 'Absolutely not.'

No, definitely not.

'Well,' he said, since if he was spouting this kind of nonsense, then he needed to leave. 'I will see you down at dinner in an hour.'

Then he left before she could reply.

Zoe didn't watch him go. She stared down at the gowns on the bed and struggled to hold onto her temper. The gall of him. First insisting on her wearing a gown to dinner, and *then* inviting a lover to bed on their wedding night? It shouldn't have made her so furious, especially when their marriage was on paper only, and anyway, what did she care how many lovers he had?

Yet she still found she didn't like it. She didn't like it at all. Perhaps it was merely that it was surprisingly tasteless of him to suggest it. It had to be that. It certainly wasn't because she was jealous, because why would she be? Just as she wasn't jealous of these gowns lying on the bed.

To be jealous, you had to care and she didn't care about him, not any more. He could fly in a whole group of women for naked swimming in the pool she'd spotted as they'd landed on the island, she didn't give a shit.

You do care, come on.

She pulled a face and picked up one of the gowns, the silver one he'd suggested. It was silver net with a black silk underdress and it was quite pretty, if she was honest about it. But he'd said he thought it would look lovely on her, and so she couldn't wear it. A pity, because it was the most modest of the lot.

She didn't wear sexy dresses. She didn't wear dresses, full stop, or sexy clothes of any description. It was jeans and T-shirts all the way for her. But he'd insisted on this stupid dressing up rule, and while she could have turned up in her usual gear, part of her didn't want to. Mainly because that was what he was likely expecting her to do, she was sure.

Surprising him, perhaps even shocking him, would be far more satisfying.

Well, then. You know what to do, don't you?

Zoe picked up the black dress. It was slinky and formfitting, but the red was…eye-catching. She picked that one up and surveyed it. It had a slit in the skirt that went almost up to her hip, the tiniest straps she'd ever seen and a deep cowl neck that was as indecent as the thigh slit.

He would definitely *not* expect her to wear that one, which meant she absolutely had to wear that one.

Nothing to do with the heat in his eyes that you saw up in the plane.

Zoe shoved that thought out of her head. It was dangerous in ways she couldn't quite pinpoint and she didn't want to be thinking about it. She wanted to shock him, that was all, and the red dress would definitely shock him.

Carefully, she laid the dress back down onto the bed before having a cursory poke around the room, annoyed to find that she liked it. It really was pretty with the whitewashed walls and the gauzy curtains around the bed.

She didn't have anything much to unpack, so she went straight into the bathroom for a shower, and was irritated to find that she liked the bathroom, too. The walls were tiled in bright handcrafted tiles and there was a huge stone bath she decided she'd definitely use at some point.

In the meantime, the big walk-in shower sufficed. Both the temperature and pressure were perfect, and she could have stood under the water all night. Especially since there were hand-milled goat's milk soaps in it that smelled absolutely delicious—notes of ambergris, cedar and, if she wasn't much mistaken, jasmine—and complementary body lotions too.

As she got out of the shower, she was again highly annoyed by how nice everything was, and the one precious thing she'd brought with her—a personal scent that she'd made herself—layered beautifully with the soaps and lotions. It was as if he'd known what kind of scents she liked and bought accordingly, which was nonsense. Archimedes was highly unlikely to have personally chosen the soaps and lotions in the damn bathroom.

Once she was clean and smelling the way she liked, she wriggled into the scarlet silk dress, appalled to find that her cotton knickers showed, no matter how she arranged the fabric, the cheerful bunnies on them completely at odds with the sexy vibe of the dress.

She scowled at the offending underwear, then slipped her knickers and bra off and stood in front of the full-length mirror in the wardrobe. A different woman stared back at her. The silk gown clung to the shape of her body, the deep neckline highlighting the curves of her breasts, the bias cut of the silk hugging her hips and then that thigh slit that went almost to her hip.

Zoe scowled at the woman in the mirror, too. It wasn't her vibe, not at all. She was used to being in the shadows, the unknown threat slipping under firewalls and getting around passwords. She wasn't used to being the centre of attention, still less in a sexual way. But this dress was deeply sexual and it made her look deeply sexual too, and she was uncomfortable about it. She also knew that if she wanted to shock Archimedes, this was how to do it.

Are you sure you want to do this?

No, she wasn't, not at all. She could take the dress off and go downstairs to dinner in her jeans and T-shirt. Or she could stay in her room and wait to see if he'd send a security guard to get her, which she was sure he would. Again, though, if she came down in jeans and a T-shirt, she knew what would happen then. He'd give her a satisfied smile and make some quip about her general loathing of dresses, which would end with her wanting to punch him in the face. But swanning downstairs with a hip-high slit in her dress, lipstick and heels would be the equivalent of a punch to his face, and had the added bonus of not hurting her fist.

So, steeling herself, Zoe kept the dress on and her underwear off, found the matching sky-high stiletto sandals that went with the dress, then teetered back into the bathroom for make-up. She had only the vaguest idea of how to put make-up on since she never wore it, but after a few attempts she managed to apply some mascara and the required lipstick. No surprises that the lipstick matched the dress too.

He'd also specified jewellery, and there were quite a few extravagant pieces in a velvet-lined drawer in the wardrobe. She never wore jewellery either, and was tempted to ignore the stipulation, but again, it would be worth the ignominy of doing what he said if it shocked the pants off him.

After a couple of minutes debating, she decided to wear the most expensive, most extravagant-looking piece she could find, whether it matched the dress or not, eventually settling on a gold choker. It was fashioned as a golden net studded with different precious stones that gleamed like tropical fish.

Once she'd put that on, she took one final look at herself in the mirror, shocked by the stranger staring back at her. She looked like someone's trophy wife, and on reflection, that was exactly what she was, which didn't help her temper. But he was the one who'd demanded this nonsense of her, so she was going to make sure she rendered him utterly speechless.

At the designated time, she left the bedroom, making her way downstairs to find a pleasant-faced older woman waiting at the bottom of the stairs. The woman introduced herself as Lydia, Mr Athineos's housekeeper, and she was here to show Zoe to dinner.

Zoe followed her through a series of corridors and down some stairs before they came out of the villa and into the warm Greek night. The air felt soft on her skin and smelled of salt and sun, with hints of warm stone and rosemary, and something tight inside her calmed. It was different to the sharp smells of London, wet concrete and rain and petrol fumes. Much more restful, and again annoyance tugged at her. She didn't want to find any of this pleasant or restful, especially when she'd been dragged here very much against her will.

Lydia led her down some stone steps to a terrace that faced the sea. Tall pines surrounded the terrace and there were lots of stone pots overflowing with lavender and rosemary. A table stood in the middle and it had been set with a white tablecloth, crystal glasses and silver cutlery. Small tea lights had been lit in exquisite glass holders made out of different coloured glass. The tiny flames leapt and danced, flickering in their holders and making the terrace look as if it was surrounded by a cloud of glowing multicoloured fairies.

It was, unfortunately, beautiful.

A tall figure stood at the edge of the terrace, looking out to sea, his hands on the parapet, and for a moment Zoe stared at his broad back, her heart beating faster. Silly of her. It was only Archimedes and she didn't care that he was wearing exquisitely tailored evening clothes that seemed to highlight every line of his powerful shoulders and narrow waist. She didn't care what he thought of her in the gown, either. All that mattered was that she shocked him or unsettled him in some way, that was all.

'Mrs Athineos, sir,' Lydia said, then withdrew back up the stairs.

Zoe lifted her chin, ignoring the strange bolt of electricity that had gone through her at the mention of 'Mrs Athineos'. Which of course she was, not that she'd ever call herself that.

Archimedes turned and a wave of intense satisfaction swept through her as his eyes went wide, taking her in, a ripple of shock flickering over his handsome face.

She lifted her chin higher, meeting his gaze head-on.

'Well?' she said. 'Here I am. Gown, shoes, jewellery and lipstick, as specified.'

His gaze flickered then travelled down her body, taking in every inch of her, and, much to her horror, she found herself blushing yet again. What was going on? Satisfaction that she'd managed to shock him, yes. Blushing because he was very definitely looking at her body and was no doubt aware that she wasn't wearing any underwear? Definitely not.

Perhaps she should have kept her cotton knickers on.

Slowly, Archimedes's gaze travelled back up to her face once more, a deep blue spark gleaming in his eyes. A spark that sent prickles of heat all over her skin.

He, of course, looked magnificent in black. Dark and dangerous, a beautiful threat, and she wished she wasn't so aware of him in that way. She wished that all those hot prickles weren't what she had a horrible feeling they were.

Without taking his gaze from hers, he walked over to her with the lithe grace of a stalking panther, before stopping and holding out his hand.

'Mrs Athineos,' he said. 'Let me escort you to the table.'

Zoe didn't want to be escorted anywhere or to take his hand, a very feminine part of her knowing that touching him would make that prickling sensation worse, make her heart beat much faster than it already was. Make her want things she most definitely didn't want.

She could still feel his mouth brushing over hers when he'd kissed her in the church and the warm touch of his skin as he'd slid his ring on her finger. Yes, touching him would be a very, *very* bad idea. Which meant her only option was to ignore his hand, brush past him and sit down at the table herself. However, doing that would mean betraying the fact that she didn't want to touch him, and she could already tell he knew that already. That he was challenging her to touch him, daring her to.

He'd done that to her as a child, encouraging her out of her comfort zone, daring her to push her own boundaries, to learn more, to do things she didn't think she could do or was afraid of. The first time she'd successfully hacked into a Fortune 500 company's mainframe was because he'd dared her to, and when she'd done it he'd been just as pleased for her as she was for herself.

This kind of challenge, though, was of a different sort and one she wasn't used to, but she knew already that she couldn't refuse it. She couldn't back down or show him any kind of weakness, because he was just as aware as she was of how a weakness in any kind of defences could be exploited.

So, bracing herself, Zoe very deliberately placed her fingers in his and, ignoring the sharp jolt of electricity that pulsed through her at the touch, she let him lead her to her seat.

CHAPTER FIVE

ARCHIMEDES COULD NOT remember the last time the sight of a woman in a dress had shocked him the way seeing Zoe swathed in scarlet silk had shocked him. When he'd had Lydia put out the gowns, he'd already decided that she wouldn't choose the scarlet one because it flashed too much skin. He'd been hoping for the little black dress because it was clingy, but this? He couldn't have asked for better.

Zoe Hargreaves hadn't just blossomed. She was a rose in full bloom.

The scarlet silk clung to the most perfect hourglass figure, hugging her breasts, hips and thighs in the sexiest way possible. Her mouth was a lush bow of red, the gold choker making her neck look long and swanlike.

And that wasn't even taking in the fact that she wasn't wearing any underwear. The thin straps holding up the scarlet silk were the only things over her shoulders and there was no incriminating fabric showing through the hip-high slit in the fabric. No, there was nothing but a swathe of pale, bare skin.

He even had to confess to being a little stunned, which had never happened to him before.

He'd spent the past hour making sure the table had been set the way he wanted it, and that the chef had prepared the food to his satisfaction. She'd agreed to this dinner at least, and since he didn't know if she would agree to more, he'd decided to make the most of this one.

She was his wife now, and that changed things, though he wasn't sure how or why. Something to do with his ring being on her finger and the sound of her being called 'Mrs Athineos'. Also, her being a vision in red, which his body liked very, very much indeed.

He wasn't sure if she'd take his hand, but he'd offered it anyway, the devil in him, the one that liked pushing boundaries, making him present it to her. But she'd accepted his challenge and now her fingers were in his, and her skin was warm, and all he could think about was sliding his hand up her arm to those ridiculously thin straps and ripping them away so the silk would fall very slowly down and off her.

A dangerous thought. Pushing boundaries at work was one thing, but not when it came to his own personal boundaries. Those were far too easy for him to excuse and manipulate, to find reasons for pushing them the way he had when he'd been with the Russians. And he knew where that led.

He could not give in to it.

Zoe could never be part of any boundary pushing anyway, even dressed as she was in scarlet silk like a delicious present he wanted to unwrap. And not only because of his own weakness, but because he suspected she had no idea what she was doing, all dressed up like that. He'd been expecting her to turn up in jeans and a T-shirt, or even not turn up at all and he'd have to make good on his threat to send a security guard for her. But no. She was here, wearing all the things he'd specified, and maybe the mistake was his. Maybe, given his weakness, he shouldn't have made those conditions.

She didn't look at him as he led her over to her seat, letting go of her hand to pull out her chair for her.

'You don't need to do that,' she said. 'I can push my own chair in.'

He should let her sit, he really should. But that devil in him wouldn't let him.

'I'm sure you can,' he said. 'But I'm afraid I must insist. It's our wedding dinner after all.'

Her jaw tightened, but she didn't protest, making a big production of sitting down in the chair instead. It put her close to him, and he couldn't help but lean in slightly, inhaling her warm, sweet, spicy scent, watching the light play over the glossy fall of her hair, and catching a glimpse of the shadowed valley between her breasts.

He wanted to linger there behind her, prolong the moment, but that wouldn't be pushing her boundary so much as it was pushing his, and he didn't need to be pushing any further boundaries tonight.

Instead, he went over to the ice bucket, where the bottle of vintage champagne was chilling, and unwrapped it, popping the cork, then filling two crystal flutes.

'Not for me,' Zoe said repressively.

He looked at her. 'It's our wedding night. Surely you

can have one glass of champagne?' Again, he shouldn't be doing this, shouldn't be pushing, but he'd never been very good at doing what he should. He was much better at doing what he wanted.

And you know what happens when you do that.

Archimedes ignored the snide thought. Yes, he'd lost himself years ago, but he was past that now. He'd pulled himself out of that darkness, he'd found control, and one beautiful woman wasn't going to affect it. One beautiful woman wasn't going to affect *him*.

He pushed the champagne flute over to her, then took his own and sat down in the chair opposite. The candle flames leapt and flickered, the glow making her pale skin look like porcelain and her night-black hair, worn loose and over her shoulders, glossy as a raven's wing.

Despite all his resistance, the desire didn't lessen.

'Well?' she demanded without preamble. 'You wanted dinner with me so here I am. At dinner.'

'Yes, you are,' he agreed, then raised his glass. 'But first a toast. To our marriage.'

Zoe did not pick up her flute. 'Yay for us,' she said tonelessly.

He sipped at the cold, yeasty liquid, studying her.

'You can't stay angry about this for a whole year.'

'Oh, no? Watch me.'

'That's not the Zoe I knew. The Zoe I knew never held grudges.'

'The Zoe you knew is gone.' She sat back in her seat and then, obviously changing her mind, reached for her flute and took a sip of the champagne. 'I'm not her any more.'

That was patently obvious. The Zoe he knew always had a smile for him, was always willing to go on forbidden expeditions with him, which usually meant walking on Hampstead Heath or the Embankment, something that Banks had expressly told them not to do.

He'd never realised back then that he'd been lonely, not until Zoe had come into his life. She'd been his friend and his partner-in-crime, but she'd also become his moral compass. She'd shown him what kindness meant, giving coins to street-sleepers or feeding the stray cat that hung around Banks's house. Buying him his favourite chocolate bar from the corner shop instead of stealing it, which he would have done, because the shop owner was elderly and needed the money.

Where that kindness was now, he didn't know, because the woman sitting opposite him now had a hard look to her face and a grim cast to her mouth. Brittle, he'd thought in the church the day before, and that was certainly what she seemed to be. She'd once been his North Star because she glittered so brightly, but now that glitter had dimmed. He didn't like it.

'So, tell me who the Zoe you are now is,' he suggested.

'Why?' She was sitting rigidly in her chair and took another sip of her champagne, though it was really more of a gulp. 'We're not friends any more, Archimedes. We might be married and have to live together, but getting to know each other was not part of the deal.'

Oh, yes, that stubborn part of her was definitely present and correct.

'What about if I want to get to know you?' he asked idly.

'So far, all of this has very much been all about what you want,' she pointed out. 'Nothing at all has been about what I want.'

Archimedes shifted in his seat. He was restless already and he'd only just sat down. With an effort, he schooled himself into stillness.

'Then what do you want?' he asked, which he thought was a reasonable enough question, because she wasn't wrong. It had all been about what he wanted.

'Not to get married to you and not to be dragged halfway across Europe,' she said, taking another hefty gulp of her wine.

Okay, he could understand that. He could understand her anger about it, too. But she seemed very wedded to that anger, and especially at him.

She missed you, remember?

That was right, so she had. Oh, she'd denied it very categorically on the plane, but it had been that flat, categorical tone that had given her away. Besides, what other reason could she have for this hostility?

She'd asked him why he'd ignored her for so many years and while he'd replied with the same casualness with which she'd asked, perhaps he shouldn't have. Perhaps his leaving had affected her more deeply than he'd thought.

The ghosts of all those old feelings he'd had for her whispered through him once again, with regret bringing up the rear. He regretted many things in his life, but that one regret for the way he'd left her lingered.

He could feel it still, an ache just behind his ribs, but he ignored it. He couldn't give in to that ache, couldn't allow himself to even be aware of it. Regret indicated care, and neither feeling could be indulged.

Archimedes put his flute down and leaned forward. 'And yet here you are,' he said. 'Despite all that so-called dragging. So, what are you getting out of it? Or are you doing this out of some kind of misguided sense of loyalty to Banks?'

She snorted. 'Hardly. What does it matter what I'm getting out of it?'

'You're stubborn, Zoe,' he said. 'If you don't want to do something, you usually dig in, so he must have promised you something big.'

There was no give in her silver gaze, no softness. 'You're not exactly a pushover yourself, and clearly loyalty is something you have no idea about.' She lifted her glass, took another gulp, a challenging look on her face. 'He must be offering you something big too.'

Frustration at her hostility caught at him. No, this wasn't what either of them wanted, but they were doing it and they were here now. And…well, he hadn't seen her for years, and he was curious. But if he wanted to get anything at all from her, he suspected he was going to have to be the one who offered something first.

He wasn't a man who was used to backing down or surrendering, not after he'd surrendered all his critical thinking facilities, not to mention his soul, for years in the criminal underworld. So it went against all his instincts to be the first one to open up. But if that was the only way to get what he wanted from her, then he'd have to.

'You want to know what Banks offered me?' he asked. 'Nothing. He blackmailed me instead.'

Shock flickered across her face before she hid it, her black lashes veiling her gaze.

'Oh?' she said, her tone neutral. 'I wouldn't have thought that was possible.'

'It shouldn't be,' he agreed. 'But Banks has evidence of those early days when we siphoned a lot of money out of that insurance company's coffers. I deleted most of the incriminating things he had on me before I left, but I didn't know he'd printed out bank statements and screenshots and kept them in hard copy in his filing cabinet, the bastard.'

Zoe blinked but didn't say anything.

'I can't have that evidence getting out,' he went on. 'For the sake of my company, naturally. So I made him a counteroffer. I would do what he wanted and in return, he would give me any remaining evidence he had on me.'

She lifted her glass and swallowed the last mouthful of champagne. 'Why did you tell me that?' she asked after a moment. 'Is this some kind of quid pro quo?'

He let out a breath, holding onto his patience. 'Maybe,' he admitted. 'This is going to be a very long year if you're going to continue to be this hostile. I thought we should find some common ground.'

'I don't think we should.' She reached for the bottle

of champagne and poured herself another glass. 'I don't want to share any ground with you at all.'

'You're angry with me for leaving, aren't you?' he asked bluntly. It was the second time he'd asked the question, but he hadn't believed her answer the first time, and if she gave him the same answer this time, he was going to call her on it.

'Perhaps I just don't like you,' she shot back.

'You didn't not like me when we were kids.'

'Feelings change.' She lifted a shoulder and took another gulp of champagne. 'People change.'

She wasn't going to admit it, was she?

'I was going to take you,' he said, deciding to address the elephant in the room if she wouldn't. 'But Banks made it clear that if I did, he'd report me to the police and I'd go to jail. The only way I could get out was to leave you behind.' For the second time that night, shock flickered over her face, but he went on, because now he'd started, he might as well keep going. 'Perhaps I shouldn't have put my own freedom above yours, but I thought that once I'd got my life on track, I'd come back for you.'

Zoe blinked. 'But you never said—'

'Banks said he'd pass on my goodbyes to you,' he interrupted, searching her face. 'But I guess he didn't, did he?'

Her mouth was in a hard line, her gaze direct. 'No, he didn't. And I only have your word for that.'

'I should have written you a note. But I suspect Banks wouldn't have given you that either.'

She lifted a shoulder. 'So you say. But whatever. It was years ago and it doesn't matter now.'

Zoe wished her voice sounded as definite as the words that came out of her mouth. She wished that hearing he'd been going to take her with him if Banks hadn't got in the way hadn't come as quite the shock that it did. She wished she still felt the nothing for him that she kept telling herself she felt, yet…

The lines of his beautiful face were thrown into stark relief by the leaping flames of the candles. Those winged brows and high, perfect cheekbones. The proud blade of his nose and the hard line of his jaw. The blue of his eyes…

Her Demon. That was what she'd called him all the time when they'd been children. That was his handle. Everyone in the house used their handles rather than their actual names, plus 'Demon' had been easier to say than 'Archimedes'.

She didn't want him to be her Demon any more, though. She wanted to hold onto the anger and hurt that still dogged her, even after all these years. She didn't want to give him even the tiniest part of herself.

Yet he'd been the one to offer her something, and while he might expect her to give him something in return—nothing came for free and they both knew that, another lesson Banks had taught them—she didn't have to give it to him. Then again, where would this continued hostility get her? It wouldn't make her feel any better about this marriage or being here, and while she fully intended to have a separate life from his, they'd probably run into each other now and then. And that would be difficult and awkward if she continued holding onto this anger.

Also, the information he'd given her, in admitting that Banks was blackmailing him, was a pretty big admission for a man like him to make.

She let out a silent breath. The hurt and fury about the way he'd left hadn't magically disappeared on hearing that Banks had stopped him from taking her with him, but maybe they were a little less intense. He'd still put his freedom above her own and as far as coming back for her went, that obviously hadn't happened, but she could allow him a little grace. Besides, she'd always had a strong sense of fairness and her continuing to be stubborn about this wasn't fair.

'I think it does matter,' he said. 'Why else would you be so furious?'

She took another sip—or gulp, rather—of the champagne, since her mouth was very dry and the liquid was cold and delicious.

'Maybe,' she said, not wanting to talk about that particular subject right now. 'But if you want to know what he was offering me, it's money.' It wasn't a particularly graceful change of subject, but she hoped he'd let her have it.

Archimedes sat back in his chair, shifting in it, restless, the way he always used to be.

'Money for what?' he asked.

So, he was going to let her have that subject change. Good.

'For my own business,' she replied.

'What business?'

She was reluctant to tell him, but again, if she didn't, that would give what he thought about it too much weight, and she didn't want that.

'I want to start a company, or maybe an organisation, to protect people from online scams and sextortion, stuff like that.'

His expression was unreadable, but he nodded. 'Good idea. But you should have plenty of money by now. Or is Banks not paying you?'

She wouldn't allow herself to feel pleased by his 'good idea'. She just wouldn't.

'Of course he's paying me,' she said sharply, the question rubbing up against something painful she didn't want to acknowledge. 'But this would be a huge lump sum that will set me up for life.'

Archimedes didn't say anything for a moment, his gaze searching in a way that made her feel exposed. She wanted to look away, hide her discomfort so he wouldn't see it, but she didn't want to give him the satisfaction of knowing he affected her.

'If you'd accepted that job offer I made you,' he said eventually, 'you would have that company by now, not to mention being set up for life.'

Ah. So they were going to talk about his job offer, were they? The one he'd made and then, when she'd refused, he'd never followed up on. Never sent an email or a text, or even a phone call. He'd just accepted it.

What did you expect him to do?

She had never been sure. She only knew that when

he hadn't followed up on her refusal, it had hurt. It had felt like him leaving her all over again.

'So, was that you "coming back for me"?' She couldn't stop a faintly bitter edge from tingeing the words.

An expression she couldn't read crossed his face. 'I realise it was probably too little, too late.'

'And the rest.' She swallowed yet more champagne, because it was starting to hit now, and she was feeling pleasantly giddy.

'I didn't want to work for you, Archimedes. Not when it was a pity offer anyway.'

One brow shot up. 'A pity offer?' he echoed. 'You thought I was offering you a job because I felt sorry for you?'

'Well, weren't you? I don't hear from you for ten years and then suddenly, out of the blue, you send me a hard copy letter offering me a job. No phone call, no "Hi, how are you, how have you been?". Just an offer of a position.' She couldn't hide the hurt in her voice and that was probably a mistake, but she'd said it now. She couldn't take it back.

His expression suddenly became enigmatic. 'I'd planned to talk to you once you'd accepted the job. I didn't want Banks intercepting any of our emails or texts, and you know he would have. He wouldn't have wanted you accepting any other job offer either. A letter was the best way to do it.'

As much as she hated to admit it, that made sense. Banks managed to know all kinds of things that were supposedly private, because he was a manipulative old man. He would have been furious if he'd found that letter of Archimedes's. He was a jealous keeper of her skills and she'd liked that. She'd liked knowing that she mattered to someone, even if it was only for her hacking skills.

'Okay,' she allowed. 'But why did you send it in the first place?'

'Come on, Zoe,' he said, sounding impatient. 'I sent it to you because you're the best in the world at what you do. Your skills would have been invaluable to Ares and you could have named your price. I would have paid it.'

She swallowed, her throat tightening. Yes, she liked being wanted for her skills, it was true. She liked being valued for them. But even though she had only the dimmest memories of the love her parents had given her, that she'd lost when they'd died, that was what she longed for. Someone to love her for herself. And while Banks had valued her, he'd never said that he loved her, not once.

Archimedes's job offer had been cold, nor had it acknowledged that he'd left without a word—or at least that was what she'd thought. It had seemed as if he'd almost expected her to take it, the lord of the manor throwing money into the crowd for people to snatch and fight over.

'If you wanted me so badly,' she said, 'why didn't you ever follow up on it?'

'Because you were very definite in your refusal.' His tone was flat. 'Then again, you always did give your loyalty to the wrong people.'

Immediately, a hot flood of anger washed through her. Was he talking about her loyalty to Banks? Was he angry about it? Well, too bad. Banks was a difficult and complicated man, it was true, not to mention a thief, but he'd been the only adult in her life who'd seemed to care about her. Also, *he* hadn't abandoned her the way Archimedes had.

'You judgemental arsehole,' she snapped. 'What would you know about loyalty?'

A muscle jumped in the side of his jaw, his whole body tensing, and he opened his mouth to say something, but Zoe had had enough. She didn't want to hear what he had to say, so, full of champagne and an uncontainable rage, she shoved her chair back and stood up.

'Sorry, but I'm not going to sit here and listen to you get at me for sticking by a man who's been a father to me since I was five years old. You can go to hell.' She turned from the table without another word, heading for the steps back up to the villa.

'Zoe—' Archimedes called from behind her '—Zoe, sit down. We haven't finished.'

She ignored him.

'Zoe!'

She ignored that too.

Until a firm hand gripped her arm, stopping her in her tracks before pulling her around. Then he was there, right in front of her, looking down from his great height, his blue gaze blazing, the warmth of his hand on her skin making her breath catch.

And for a moment all they did was stare at each other, the air between them full of anger and grief, loss and regret. And a hot, vibrating thing that felt like sparks from a live wire.

She was going to pull away, she really was. At least, that was what she'd intended. Then he suddenly and firmly pulled her up against his powerful body, slid his other hand into her hair then tipped her head back, and covered her mouth with his.

Abruptly, the anger inside her alchemised into something hot and raw, something hungry, and her mouth was opening beneath his, her hands clutching at the fabric of his jacket. He tasted of the champagne they'd been drinking, effervescent and alcoholic, and it made her dizzy, made her lean into him, desperate for more. Then he was tasting her, his tongue in her mouth, exploring, ravaging, devastating. She went up on her toes, returning the kiss, the hot and hungry thing inside her becoming even hotter, even hungrier.

This was all she'd ever wanted. His kiss. His body against hers. His hand in her hair, closing into a fist as he held her still.

He was all she'd ever wanted.

His hand on her arm moved to her hip, sliding around to the small of her back, urging her more firmly against him, and she could feel the hard length of him pressing against her. It stole her breath.

The kiss became deeper, turning into something uncontrollable and wild, and he kept a firm grip on her hair as his hand moved yet again, to the slit in her dress and beneath the silk, finding the warm skin of her thigh.

Zoe made a soft sound in the back of her throat, a

moan or a gasp, she wasn't sure which, because then his hand slid around to cup the bare skin of her rear, squeezing her lightly.

Pleasure arced through her, a blinding need that she couldn't control, and her fingers tightened where they gripped his jacket, pulling him towards her.

'Demon,' she whispered against his mouth, no thought in her head, every shred of anger and hurt gone, vanishing under the sweeping wave of desire that was drowning her. 'Demon, please…'

He didn't reply, except to squeeze her again, then to turn with her and push her back against the table. He stopped kissing her long enough to sweep everything off the table, ignoring the glasses that shattered on the ground and the plates that cracked into pieces. Then he lifted her up as if she weighed nothing and sat her on the tabletop. Zoe shivered as he pushed her thighs wide, her hands reaching for him, trying to pull him close, but he was too busy undoing his trousers, finding a condom from his pocket and rolling it down.

Then finally, at last he was close, as close as she'd always longed for him to be, easing aside the silk of her gown, baring her to him. His hands slid up her thighs, gripping her tight, and then he was pushing inside her, making her cry out. He felt big and hard, and it felt as if there was no room for her, no room to breathe or even move, because he filled her. He was everywhere.

She trembled even as she felt herself stretch to fit him, and the panicky feeling eased. Then he was kissing her again, the kiss deep and hot and slow, and he began to move inside her and everything fell away.

There was nothing but the intense pleasure flooding through her, making everything brighter, everything better.

Yes, this was what she wanted, what she needed. Her Demon, as close to her as another person could get, linked to her, tangled up with her. A part of her.

She kissed him back as deeply and as hungrily as he was kissing her, trying to undo his shirt so she could get to the warm skin beneath the cotton, to touch him the way he was touching her. And he was touching her, one hand at the small of her back, beneath her dress, subtly guiding her movements, the other sliding beneath the narrow strap of her dress and easing it off her shoulder, baring one breast to his palm.

Zoe gasped again, arching into him and his touch, her eyes closing as the pleasure took hold, the relentless build of it making her moan.

She'd had no idea it could be like this. No idea that it could feel this good, this intense. But a small part of her knew already that there was a reason for that.

It was him. Because no matter how angry and hurt she was, she still trusted him. Even all these years later.

'Star,' he murmured against her lips, his mouth moving down her neck, trailing kisses everywhere. 'My beautiful star.'

She wrapped her legs around his waist, the soft sound of her old handle and nickname making her ache. But then he was moving faster, harder, and the whole world became the pleasure he was intensifying, the friction making her pant, making her plead.

Then he dropped one hand between her thighs and

touched her just where she needed it most, and the tight knot that had been slowly tightening inside her came undone, raw pleasure flooding her.

She cried his name, only dimly aware that he was moving even faster, before abruptly, he turned his face against her throat and groaned her name as he followed her over the edge.

CHAPTER SIX

ARCHIMEDES COULDN'T DO anything but stand there, leaning against the edge of the table, holding Zoe in his arms as she trembled and shook with the aftershocks of her orgasm. For the first time in his life, his mind was blank. There was nothing in his head, no chatter, no noise. Only peace.

He wanted to stay like that forever.

But he couldn't, because as his consciousness gradually returned, he became aware of what had just happened, and who it had happened with.

After all the deals he'd made with himself, after all his protestations, he'd forgotten each and every one of them and done exactly what he was *not* supposed to do. He'd let his own desire get the better of him, and not only that but his temper too.

He'd told himself for years that her refusal of his job offer didn't matter to him, that he didn't care, but her telling him that it had only been a pity offer, that he didn't want her really, had felt like a slap in the face. He hadn't followed up on it because she'd been very clear she didn't want him to, and so he'd left it at that.

He wasn't going to force her to work for him if she didn't want to.

Except that wasn't the only thing you were annoyed about, was it?

No, he had to admit it wasn't. A deeply buried part of him, a part of himself he never acknowledged because he didn't like people having power over him, was that he'd also been hurt. Once he'd put his ten years in the criminal underworld behind him, he'd thought—hoped even—that she might leave Banks, and come to him.

Except she never had. She'd stayed with Banks, refused his job offer, and yes, that pissed him off and it hurt. More than he'd ever wanted to admit to, and so he'd lost his temper with her, with her hostility and her barbed questions, and had said something he shouldn't have. Something that if he hadn't been so angry, he wouldn't have said. And she'd been rightly furious with him.

But he hadn't wanted her to leave, so when she'd shoved her chair back and started for the steps, all he'd been thinking was that she should stay. That they had to have this conversation.

Yet she'd kept on heading towards the steps, so he'd shoved his own chair back, reaching for her only to stop her, nothing more. Except when he'd closed his hand around her arm and she'd turned to him, her eyes wide, the fierce thread of desire that had been coiling tight inside him all this time abruptly snapped.

He'd looked down into that pure silver gaze, now gone dark with desire, and he'd seen the frantic beat of her pulse. Felt her silky skin beneath his fingers. And the tension in the air, the tension that had been between them from the moment she'd walked into the church, had been too much. He hadn't been able to fight it and he didn't want to. All he could see was her.

So he'd pulled her close almost without thinking about it, his hand sliding to the small of her back, fitting her against him, and she'd been so warm and she'd smelled so good. Her eyes had darkened even further, so he'd slid his hands into her hair before he knew what he was doing and had bent to take that delicious mouth of hers.

Just a taste, that was all he'd wanted. Only a taste. But he hadn't counted on her hunger. Because as soon as he'd kissed her, she'd risen up on her toes to kiss him back, even hotter, even hungrier. She'd taken fistfuls of his jacket, her mouth tasting of champagne and something sweet and tart, and he didn't want to stop. He didn't ever want to stop.

So he hadn't. He'd slid his hand beneath the red silk of her dress to find the satin of her skin instead, so soft and smooth under his fingers. She'd made the sexiest little sound in the back of her throat, and the control he'd been desperately holding onto shattered into pieces.

He'd had her on top of the table, spreading her legs and pushing inside her even before he'd had time to draw breath. Feeling her around him had been so unbelievably good. She'd been all tight, liquid heat, so very, very perfect. *She* was perfect. In every single way.

He'd always been a generous lover and he made sure

his partners always found satisfaction, but he hadn't been thinking with Zoe. Nothing was more important than chasing the intoxicating pleasure he was finding with her. Her softness and heat and scent. The tight feel of her around him. The sounds she made as he moved, and the clasp of her thighs around his waist. It had only been at the very last minute that he'd thought of her pleasure too, and had managed to send her over first before the orgasm had taken him, but it had been a near run thing. He'd been like a teenage boy with his first lover.

Humiliating, you realise that, don't you? After everything you told yourself.

An icy feeling wound through him, along with memories he didn't want in his head. Memories of all those years he'd spent relentlessly pursuing status and pleasure and power. Dark, terrible memories that made him feel ashamed of everything he'd done, of how he'd let himself be at the mercy of his own addictive brain.

Control was everything and he could not lose it, and yet…

She made you lose it for the first time in a decade.

Archimedes shoved himself away from her, his heart beating suddenly far too fast. She made another of those soft sounds, maybe of shock or protest, he wasn't sure which, but as he dealt with the condom and straightened, doing his trousers back up, he found her watching him. Her gaze was wide and shocked, still dark with pleasure, and her cheeks were flushed. She looked so beautiful, his heart felt sore in his chest.

He should say something, give her some reassurance at least, because given her unpractised response to him, he didn't think she was all that experienced. Yet, perhaps for the first time in his life, he couldn't think of a word to say.

You can't leave her like that, not her.

Shame rose up in him then, hot and bitter, because he knew he'd crossed a line, a line he'd sworn to himself that he'd never cross. This wasn't just some woman he'd had on the tabletop, this was *Zoe*. His North Star. His foster sister.

Also your wife, don't forget.

He took a breath, restlessness filling every part of him, the urge to move, to turn around and leave so strong he could barely resist it. But he made himself stay there, looking into her eyes.

'Are you okay?' he asked, forcing the words out. 'Did I hurt you?'

She said nothing, her gaze searching his.

'Zoe,' he prompted, her name edged with an impatience he couldn't hide. 'Answer me.'

She blinked and looked away, the colour in her cheeks rising as she pushed herself off the table, smoothing down her dress.

'Yes,' she said, her voice husky. 'I'm fine.'

She wasn't fine, though, he could hear that too.

Do something, you fucking idiot.

But doing something would mean touching her again, and if he knew one thing all too well, it was that he couldn't touch her again. She was a weakness, a flaw in his otherwise flawless control, and now he had to be on his guard around her. He could not, whatever he did, get close to her again.

'Good,' he said, adjusting his jacket and then, because he couldn't keep himself standing there a second longer, he continued. 'Please feel free to eat. I have a number of things to do, so if you'll excuse me—'

He didn't wait for her to respond. He simply turned around and went back up the steps to the villa. She didn't say anything, didn't call his name, and he was glad of that, because he wasn't sure what he'd do if she had.

There was a gym in one wing of the villa and he headed straight there, pausing only to change into more appropriate clothing, before stepping inside and going straight to the treadmill. Then he put it on its toughest program and threw himself into working out the restless, wired energy that crackled in his blood.

He had failed himself. He had given in. And he knew what happened when he did that. If he kept giving in, if he kept surrendering to his appetites, he'd become that monster again, addicted to the rush of power and status and excess. A monster Zoe would run a mile from, if he didn't drag her down with him first.

The past he'd left behind wasn't gone. There was still a hunger in him, a restlessness that made him unable to keep still or stay in one place for too long. A need for new challenges, new thrills—new anything. He funnelled all that restless energy into his work and into staying in control of himself and his hungers. And he managed them. He kept a stranglehold on his control at all times, and for years now he'd stayed that way.

Yet within the space of a day, since meeting Zoe again, all those lessons he'd learned had been forgotten, all his good intentions burned to the ground.

It was unconscionable, and he only had himself to blame.

From now on, he had to be better. He had to stay on the right side of the line he'd drawn in the sand, and he couldn't cross back over it.

She was a temptation he couldn't afford to be around, both for his own sake and for hers. Because if there was one thing he knew without a doubt, it was that he would never, ever allow himself to drag her down into the dark with him.

Zoe made her way slowly back up the steps from the terrace where she'd lost her virginity. Shock as well as pleasure were still echoing through her as she headed towards the villa, though right at that moment all she could think about was the look in Archimedes's blue eyes after he'd pushed himself away from her and then had stood there, looking at her.

She had seen her own shock reflected in his gaze, as well as a fury she didn't understand. His eyes had blazed, his whole body drawn tight with tension, even after that orgasm. She'd had no idea what to say, no idea how to bridge the distance that had abruptly sprung up between them, and he hadn't given her any hints either. He'd merely issued a stiff invitation to eat, before turning round and making his way back up the steps.

Her emotions felt raw, as if her nerve-endings had been exposed and every little breath of air caused them pain, and she wasn't sure if she should be furious with him for walking away or glad that he'd given her privacy to process what had happened between them.

You're not angry or relieved. You're hurt.

A lump rose in her throat as she walked slowly back up the steps, every muscle feeling shaky and sore, and no matter how many times she blinked there were still tears in her eyes.

She didn't want to be hurt that he'd walked away. She didn't want to feel anything but mildly pleased about losing her virginity. But no matter how many times she told herself that, an ache behind her breastbone gave the lie to her rationalisation.

He'd turned her world upside down in every single way there was, and then, after only a cursory question about whether she was okay or not, he'd walked away as if what had happened between them had meant nothing.

Zoe angrily swiped the tears from her eyes as she neared the villa, before swallowing the rest down. She was *not* going to cry about it and she was *not* going to cry about him either, not when she'd shed so many tears over him already.

They'd had sex, yes, and it had been amazing, but now that was out of the way, they could get on with their separate lives. It didn't have to change anything, and she would make sure that it didn't. Not that there was anything to change. They didn't have any kind of relationship these days except their on-paper marriage anyway, so there was really nothing to be upset about.

Once inside the villa, Zoe headed up to her bedroom

and then went straight into the bathroom. She ran herself a nice hot bath with a little bit of the gorgeous-smelling bath oil, since she was a little sore, and once the tub was full she slipped out of her dress and into the water.

Then she lay back and stared up at the ceiling, letting the warmth of the water and the scent of the bath oil soothe her aching muscles and any lingering soreness. The lump in her throat refused to go away, though, and her brain refused to stop replaying the feel of him inside her, his hands on her skin, his hot mouth on hers. And then that shocked look…

Zoe blinked as something occurred to her in that moment. Yes. He'd been *shocked.* As if he hadn't been expecting that to happen as much as she hadn't. Almost, even, as if he'd been so overcome by desire for her that he hadn't been able to help himself.

She blinked again, heat moving through her that had nothing to do with the temperature of the water, and with it came something else.

Wonder.

She didn't like admitting how powerless she'd felt over the years, held to ransom in a way by her own sense of loyalty to Banks, and to a pain that had been sitting unacknowledged in her heart for a long time. She'd always thought that her hacking skills were her special power, but even those were in service to someone else, and she'd often wondered what Banks would do if she ever lost them for some reason. Would he get rid of her? Abandon her? She'd never wanted to test the theory, so she'd stayed. Because at least she still meant something to Banks.

But it came to her suddenly that she wasn't powerless, not here and not with Archimedes, because she had the power to unsettle him. She had the power to affect him, to shock him, to make him lose his control, and that was something she'd never anticipated.

And she had. At dinner she'd needled him, making him shift in his seat, making anger flicker in his gaze. Then she'd made him come after her and the moment he'd laid a hand on her she'd made him lose all control of himself. He'd had her on the table with only the modicum of forethought with the condom.

The tight sensation in her chest eased, the lump in her throat slowly disappearing. She'd hadn't realised that tonight she'd been testing her power over him, with her dress and her body, and all his self-command had come crashing down, so…why not do more with it?

Why not torture him with it? Get him back for all the years he'd tortured her. Make him burn the way she'd burned.

Are you sure that's a good idea? Sounds like a recipe for disaster if you're not careful.

Yes, that was true. It would be better if she could remain unaffected, but she had enough insight to know that wasn't the case. She was as much at the mercy of her desire for him as he was for her, and this plan could very well backfire on her if so.

Then again, her plan backfiring would only mean surrendering to her own hunger, and that would end up being very pleasurable for her, so why not? She'd missed out on a lot growing up, since Banks had been very strict and she hadn't wanted to do anything to upset him in case he sent her straight back into the foster system. So why couldn't she take a little something for herself? She had to live here for a year, and sure, she could ship some guy in, but it would be so much easier to have the guy already here. The one guy she trusted enough to give her body to, at least.

A thrill of excitement arrowed through her, and she nearly got out of the tub, ready to go and find him immediately. But no, she shouldn't rush this. She had to leave him to his shock, and while that might mean he'd be on his guard around her even more now, it would be interesting to test it.

He was surrounded by the impregnable firewall of his own control, but she was good at getting past firewalls. She was good at finding weaknesses, at slipping through the cracks undetected, and she was sure she could find his.

Zoe smiled at the ceiling then slipped under the water to wash her hair.

CHAPTER SEVEN

ARCHIMEDES HAD A full schedule. First, he had a project to check in on at his New York office, then he had meetings in Washington, Tokyo and Shanghai, so staying on Kythea was definitely not what he'd intended.

Yet he found himself waking up the next morning, his body aching, his cock hard, and the urge to find Zoe burning like a fire in his blood.

He'd run himself ragged on the treadmill the night before, then had lifted more weights than he should have, so no wonder his body ached. But there was nothing else to explain his desperate physical desire except her.

Perhaps if he'd decided to have Celeste visit, things would have been better, but after he'd had Zoe on the dinner table, the thought hadn't even occurred to him.

It occurred to him now, though, as he stalked downstairs in search of coffee, except sadly the moment had passed and the thought of her now no longer interested him. Just as the thought of boarding his Gulfstream and flying to the US no longer interested him.

It was ludicrous and it had never happened before that something could, or even would, distract him from work, but apparently ludicrous things happening had entered his life and were causing havoc.

The ludicrous things being Zoe.

A breakfast table had been laid on the upper terrace, so he went out to grab a cup of coffee, part of him tightening at the thought of seeing her there. Only for that part to twist with what he refused to acknowledge was disappointment when he found she wasn't. Perhaps she was upstairs still asleep. Perhaps she'd had as bad a night's sleep as he had.

Not that you can blame her after the way you left things.

A muscle twitched in Archimedes's jaw as he poured himself some of the thick black Greek coffee he preferred. He didn't want to think about his behaviour the night before after his spectacular loss of control, or the shock in her darkening silver eyes. He didn't want to admit that he'd treated her appallingly, with far less care and understanding than he'd treat one of his other lovers, and he certainly didn't want to admit that he felt bad about it.

He didn't want to admit to, or to feel, anything at all.

That way lay destruction, as he well knew, so really, the only option for him was to get on his bloody jet and get the hell back to work.

Except he didn't. He sipped moodily at his coffee, staring out at the ocean instead. At least until he heard a footstep behind him. He turned to see Zoe step out onto the terrace and everything in him tightened.

Her black hair was loose down her back and glossy in the morning sun, and she was wearing a very sheer kaftan of white cotton that did nothing at all to hide the fact that she was wearing a very small red bikini underneath it.

He remembered that bikini. He'd ordered it in along with the gowns, though, like the red gown, he'd assumed she'd never wear it. Except she was very definitely wearing it now and the sight of her in it turned his blood to liquid fire.

It was a string bikini, with nothing but small triangles cradling her breasts and another hiding the soft, dark curls he'd felt the night before, leaving the rest of her delicious curves utterly bare.

'Good morning,' she said cheerfully as she came over to the table, not even looking at him as she reached for the coffee pot, too. 'I hope you slept well.'

Archimedes gritted his teeth, fighting the very real desire to go to her, rip aside that kaftan along with her bikini, sweep all the breakfast dishes away and have her on this table, too.

'Yes,' he bit out, trying to dredge up some politeness from somewhere. 'Did you?'

She finally looked at him, her silver eyes glinting with something he didn't recognise. 'Very well, thank you.'

'Good.' The word came out sounding wooden, so he shut his mouth on anything else he was going to say, and continued to sip at his coffee. He shouldn't look at her, that was the issue. He should finish his coffee, say goodbye, then get in his jet and go to his bloody meetings, not stand there staring at her.

But he didn't.

A very small, very faint smile turned one corner of her mouth, and he found himself staring it. How long had it been since he'd got a smile from her? Not since he'd left. But now, here she was, giving him a ghost of a smile, and he could feel the effect of it echo throughout his entire body. He wanted more, he wanted the real Zoe smile he remembered, open and generous and only for him, not this…whatever it was. Because this wasn't her usual smile, not with that look of calculation in her eyes.

A flicker of anger caught him. The one thing Zoe had never been was calculating. She'd always been honest and clear about what she wanted and what she thought, and the look in her eyes was unfamiliar to him. Or no, it was familiar. He'd seen it in Banks's eyes, too.

'See something funny?' he asked, unable to keep the temper from his voice.

'Yes.' The ghost of a smile continued to play around her mouth, her eyes glinting. 'Or rather, *I'm* amused.'

The muscle in the side of his jaw twitched again. 'What about?'

Though he was starting to get an inkling, oh, yes, he was getting there. Zoe wouldn't normally wear a bikini like that, which meant she was wearing it for a reason. And that reason was likely to torture him, especially after last night.

She shrugged and sipped at her own coffee. 'Oh, nothing in particular.'

'If you want an apology for last night, just say it,' he snapped, losing patience.

'I don't want an apology,' she said. 'Do you?'

His anger spat and crackled like a live wire. 'Stop playing games, Zoe. We both know why you're wearing that bikini.'

'Do we?' She raised a brow. 'I thought I was wearing it because I wanted to go for a swim, but clearly you have other ideas.'

Archimedes took a breath, struggling to keep hold of his temper. The scales had tipped in an indefinable way and he didn't like it one bit. He was used to being in charge of his life and everything in it, and yet one day and a night since Zoe had returned and he was somehow losing his grip on his command. That couldn't happen, he refused to allow it.

'I'm flying to the States today,' he said crisply, trying to take control of the conversation. 'I'll be away a few weeks. If you need anything, please ask Lydia and she'll assist you.'

'Fine,' she said, as if him leaving was no big deal. 'You do get very formal when you're angry, did you know that?'

His jaw was tight. Every part of him was tight.

'I'm not angry,' he said through his teeth. 'Whatever gave you that idea?'

'Oh, nothing. Except you look like you're ready to chew your way through a stone wall.'

A hot spark glowed in her silver eyes, a glint that made him take an unconscious step towards her as his patience gradually slipped through his fingers, along with the rest of his temper. And she noticed, of course she did, because she put her cup down and turned away.

'Have a nice few weeks,' she said over her shoulder. 'Don't miss me too much.' Then she walked back down the stone steps that led to the pool area without looking back, the warm breeze making her kaftan billow and wrap around her luscious figure.

Archimedes couldn't stand it, and he couldn't stand still any longer, so he started walking. He really did mean to go back into the villa to prepare for his trip, except he found himself following her down the steps to the pool area instead, watching as she stopped by one of the sun loungers and pulled her kaftan over her head. Her body was pale as porcelain, her skin silky and smooth as milk.

She must have heard him coming because she tossed a glance over her shoulder, her gaze meeting his. 'I thought you were going to the States,' she said.

'I am.' He continued walking, going over to the sun lounger where she stood. 'In a minute.'

One of her dark brows rose, the glint in her eyes making him burn to show her exactly how dangerous playing these kinds of games with him was. Especially when he was this on edge.

'And what are you going to do for that minute? Have a quick swim? Because if so, you're not dressed for it.'

'That can easily be remedied.' He held her gaze. 'Don't play with me, Zoe.' His voice had dropped and he was unable to stop a growl from entering it. 'You wouldn't like the consequences.'

'I'm not playing any game,' she said, her chin lifting. 'I'm just going for a swim.'

No, she wasn't. She was doing this deliberately and

it had nothing to do with swimming. But while she might have an idea of what kind of game she thought she was playing, he knew without a doubt, and it was not a game she should play with him.

So? Turn around. Go back to the villa and get on that fucking jet.

He should, he really should. But she was looking at him, daring him, and so instead, he casually lifted his hands to the buttons of his crisp white shirt and began undoing them. Zoe's gaze wavered, a fleeting look of surprise crossing her face.

Good. Two could play that game, and he was a master at it. As she would soon find out. He wasn't going to do anything more, of course. He was only going to tease her a little before leaving for his trip.

He didn't rush. He undid the buttons of his shirt slowly before pulling it off, leaving his chest bare. Her gaze drifted over his shoulders and chest, down to his abs and, satisfyingly, colour rose in her cheeks.

'What are you doing?' she asked, her voice husky.

'You said I wasn't dressed for swimming.' He tossed the shirt down on the sun lounger before getting rid of his shoes. 'And you were right.' He dropped his hands to his belt. 'So I'm solving the issue.'

She blinked. Rapidly. 'You've got swimming trunks on though, haven't you?'

Archimedes unzipped his trousers then pulled them down, along with his boxers.

'No.' He tossed the rest of his clothing down on the lounger along with his shirt. 'When I swim, I swim naked.'

Zoe had now gone as red as her bikini, her eyes very wide as she stared at him. And she *did* stare at him. At all of him.

He lifted a brow, satisfaction coiling inside him at her blush and the glitter of appreciation in her eyes. 'See something you like?'

She hurriedly averted her gaze from his body. But it was too late. They both knew she'd stared, and now they both knew she'd definitely liked what she saw.

'No.' The huskiness in her voice was pronounced now. 'Of course not. If I'd known you were going to swim—'

'Naked,' he finished for her. 'If you'd known I was going to swim naked, then what would you have done, Zoe? Please, enlighten me.'

The red glow in her cheeks had spread down her neck and chest, the bikini she wore hiding nothing. 'I would have decided not to swim.' Her chin took on a stubborn slant, even though she was staring at the water. 'In fact, maybe I've changed my mind—'

'Coward,' Archimedes interrupted, low and rough. 'You started this game. You wanted to play it. But now you're getting pushback, you don't like it? That's not the Zoe I knew. The Zoe I knew had the guts to follow through at least.'

She looked at him sharply, anger flickering in her eyes. But he didn't wait for her to respond. She'd made the first move and he'd countered it. The next move was hers.

Archimedes turned, strode over to the edge of the pool and dived in.

* * *

Zoe watched his sleek tanned figure dive neatly into the water, all the while silently berating herself. She'd felt so smug this morning, dressing in the bikini and throwing a kaftan over the top, looking forward to seeing his reaction before he left for whatever trip he was going on. Then she was going to settle herself in front of her computer and work on figuring out how to breach the Ares firewalls.

When she'd come down to breakfast and found him standing with a cup of coffee and staring moodily into the distance, her heart had beat a little faster, she couldn't lie. She'd had a terrible sleep the night before, her dreams full of him, but she'd hauled herself out of bed, determined to put him in his place with the plan she'd decided on.

She'd steeled herself for his presence, of course, but still, seeing him standing there in a crisp white business shirt and tailored dark blue trousers, his eyes glowing fiercely, had made her breath catch. Then it had caught again when their gazes had met and his had widened, taking in what she was wearing.

A charge of satisfaction had gone through her, which had only deepened after it became obvious that he was in a temper, and probably because of how she affected him. She'd had to smile at that, which had only annoyed him more.

Of course, he knew what game she was playing—he was too experienced not to—but she'd had fun pretending she wasn't playing games at all, pushing his temper further. He was leaving, as he'd said, and wouldn't be back for weeks, so why not push him for all she was worth?

She'd thought she'd had the last laugh when she'd turned away to go to the pool, but apparently he'd had other ideas. She hadn't expected him to follow her to the pool area, only seeing he'd followed her after taking her kaftan off.

She'd had to brazen it out, because her plan had only extended to needling him before he left. She hadn't thought about what to do if he made a move, and she certainly hadn't counted on him not leaving at all.

She hadn't counted on him using the same tactics she'd used on him to get to her either. The lazy way he'd unbuttoned his shirt, his blue gaze holding hers, before taking it off, exposing broad shoulders, muscled chest and hard, carved abs. His skin was the deep olive of his homeland, and smooth, crisp black hair curled on his chest. He was the most beautiful man she'd ever seen and her mouth had dried. Then it had dried even further as he'd unbuttoned his trousers and stepped free of his clothes. He'd stood in front of her, gloriously naked and not caring one bit, not that he had any reason to care since he was magnificent, but there had been definite challenge in his eyes.

He's right though, isn't he? You are *a coward.*

Anger clenched inside her as she watched him surface, his black hair sleek as a seal's pelt. He'd taken the one advantage she'd had over him and had called her bluff, raised the stakes, and she didn't know if she was equipped to answer it.

Archimedes lifted a hand and ran it through his wet

black hair, glancing over his shoulder at her. Water glistened on his skin, drops trailing down his powerful shoulders and back, and hunger twined with the anger sitting like a hot coal inside her.

She'd decided she was going to push him, but she should have expected that he wouldn't wait around to make a move. He'd always been a man of decisive action, who took control of a situation, and that hadn't changed. Neither had the way he challenged her.

You always met his challenges back then. Are you going to run away now?

Zoe drew in a silent breath. Back when she'd been an anxious little girl, he was the one who'd drawn her out of her shell, who'd encouraged her to do the things that scared her, that she was nervous of, and each and every time she'd overcome some obstacle he'd cheered her on. He was the one who'd helped her to be better, to be great, not Banks, and he was doing the same thing now.

The contrary, stubborn part of her could not let it go. Could not let him be right that she was every bit the coward he accused her of being. Because she wasn't a coward. She wasn't.

Aren't you? Isn't that why you stayed with Banks instead of leaving?

Zoe shoved that thought away hard, and slowly walked to the edge of the pool. Archimedes turned to face her, blue gaze glinting.

No, she wasn't going to walk away. She'd decided to play this game with him, and she'd acknowledged last night that it had the opportunity to backfire on her, and it was likely going to do so now. But that didn't matter.

What mattered was that his control wasn't as impregnable as it seemed—why else would he have followed her? Taken off his clothes and jumped into the water?

'You're having a swim before work?' she asked.

He lifted one muscled shoulder. 'Why not? I'm the CEO of the company. I can do whatever the hell I like.'

'You'd better step aside then,' she said. 'You're in my way.' And she reached to undo the tie of her bikini top, ignoring the nervousness that coiled tightly inside her. He'd seen most of her body anyway, since the bikini basically hid nothing, but still, being naked in front of him made her feel exposed. She wasn't going to let that get to her though, as she let her bikini top fall and shoved down her bikini bottoms. Then she straightened, watching as his gaze flared in response.

Goosebumps rose all over her bare skin, little electric shivers shocking her. There was hunger in his gaze, as well as appreciation and desire, and she found herself standing straighter, her nervousness dropping away along with the sense of exposure.

He liked looking at her and he didn't hide it, didn't bother to pretend he didn't feel it, and that felt powerful. That made her feel strong and in control, a feeling that only grew as he slowly came through the water towards her, his hungry gaze on hers.

'What are you waiting for?' His deep voice had gone even deeper, even rougher. 'The pool's big enough for both of us.'

Zoe didn't look away, her sense of power only growing at how his eyes had darkened. 'I'm just deciding whether or not I can be bothered,' she said casually, wanting to torture him, because she knew as soon as she touched the water all bets were off.

But he clearly wasn't in the mood to be tortured. He strode to the end of the pool, put his hands on the edge and pushed himself out in one smooth, athletic display of strength. And for a second Zoe wondered what would happen if she ran, and if he would chase her, but then he was there, naked and dripping wet. He reached for her, and she gasped at the touch of his cool skin against hers, then she was being lifted in his arms and carried over to the lounger.

Then she was down on it, and he was on top of her, his tall powerful figure pushing her down onto the cushions, his skin wet and slippery against hers, the cool feel of it soothing against her own heat. He settled himself between her thighs as if he had all the time in the world, and then very deliberately kissed her, light, tasting kisses that had her trembling beneath him.

It felt so good to be skin to skin, and she couldn't stop herself from running her hands over his shoulders and down his back, glorying in the feel of oiled silk beneath her fingertips. He smelled of chlorine and him, and his mouth was almost delicate on hers, as if she were a glass of the finest wine he'd ever tasted. She opened her mouth beneath his, trying to kiss him back, but he was having none of it.

'Lie still,' he ordered softly. 'You lost the game, Zoe, so now you'll have to deal with the consequences.' Then he kissed her again, deeper and slower, the complete opposite of the kiss the night before, his weight on her pinning her to the cushions, making it impossible to move. But it felt good to be pinned like this. He was an anchor, holding her to earth, making sure she didn't float away.

'Demon,' she whispered against his lips, her private name for him coming so naturally she was hardly even aware she'd said it. 'Let me touch you.'

'No,' he murmured, his mouth trailing down the side of her neck. 'Winner gets to do whatever he wants, while the loser has to lie there and take it.'

A gasp escaped her as he kept kissing down her body, his tongue tracing the curve of one breast before finding the hard point of her nipple and teasing it, nipping at it. His hands stroked, caressing her everywhere, sliding between her thighs and finding her clit, touching and teasing that too.

'Please—' she whispered again, unable to help herself, pleasure building, making her hips lift to his hand, making her shudder. 'Demon, please—' It didn't matter that she was begging, and she could hear herself do it. And it didn't matter that she was begging him. She didn't think she could keep it inside her, and anyway, he seemed to like it.

He moved down her body, his hands spreading her thighs wide, and then his mouth was between them. He licked her, nipped at the soft wet folds of her sex, nuzzled and explored her slowly and deliberately, and she couldn't stop the sounds he brought from her.

She was as lost as she'd been the night before, and she didn't care. Because he was here, giving her so much pleasure, and this was all she'd ever wanted.

Him and his touch. His kisses. His tongue and the ecstasy he gave her.

She shuddered as he brought her to the edge, but she didn't want to tip over because he hadn't taken anything for himself. He ignored her pleas. One flick of his magic tongue and the pleasure exploded through her, her cry of release echoing around the pool area.

For long moments, all she could do was lie there with her eyes closed, shaking with the aftershocks. Then she felt him shift on her. 'Don't go,' she said before she could stop herself, the words automatic and desperate.

'Don't worry,' he said as she heard the sound of foil ripping. 'I'm not going anywhere.'

Then he was between her thighs again, the blunt head of his cock pushing against her, inside her, and she groaned.

'Open your eyes,' he murmured. 'Look at me, Star.'

She didn't even think about resisting, her lashes lifting almost without thought, meeting the intense, burning blue of his gaze. He didn't speak and he didn't look away, maintaining eye contact as he began to move inside her, a slow, deliberate thrust of his hips that had her gasping.

He was beautiful, her Demon, so achingly beautiful, and she lifted her hands to his hair, burying her fingers in the damp silk of it.

'You shouldn't have left.' She didn't think about what she was saying, the words just came out. 'You should have stayed with me.'

His darkening gaze flickered then held. 'I'm here now,' he murmured. 'And so are you.'

Then he bent and covered her mouth again, kissing her hard and deep, desperate and feverish as the pleasure built and built. Until she was shaking. Until she couldn't bear it any more. Her fingers curled into fists in his hair as the orgasm broke inside her, ecstasy flooding her entire being and sending her up into space, with him following along after her.

CHAPTER EIGHT

ARCHIMEDES LAY ON Zoe's soft, warm body, again completely unable to move. Not that he wanted to even if he could. She smelled of that sweet, musky scent that drove him crazy, and her fingers were moving idly in his hair, soothing him. And yet again, his brain was blissfully empty. There was no restlessness, no desperation, no noise.

He'd made another mistake, his control failing him yet again, but in this moment he couldn't bring himself to be angry about it. Perhaps it had even been a good thing. Perhaps having sex with her would even help, since it was clear she was more temptation than he could resist.

Besides, it was only sex. He'd been making it into much more of a big deal than it needed to be. Sleeping with Zoe wouldn't send him back down that dark path again, to the place where he'd lost both himself and his morality. Anyway, he'd known the minute she'd stripped her bikini off and stood there on the edge of the pool, gloriously and beautifully naked, that his control wasn't strong enough. That he wouldn't be able to resist her no matter how hard he tried, so what was the point in trying? Better to sate this hunger to its fullest extent than to let it hollow him out inside.

He hadn't resisted. He'd got out of the pool and taken her down onto the sun lounger, and she'd been as hungry for him as he'd been for her.

But this is Zoe, *remember? She's not like any of your other lovers and you can't treat her as such.*

Oh, he was well aware, and he had no intention of treating her as such. They were married, she was his wife and they had to live together for a year, so why not start as they meant to continue? Why not satisfy their physical curiosity about each other as much as they could?

Archimedes shifted so he wasn't lying fully on top of her and lifted his head. She lay there with her black hair across the white linen of the cushions, her eyes glittering like the star he'd named her for, her cheeks beautifully and completely flushed.

He leaned one elbow on the cushion beside her, resting his head on his hand. 'Two orgasms,' he said, his voice still a little rough. 'I'm very clearly the winner.'

A smile hovered around her mouth. 'You're really arrogant, you know that?'

'Yes,' he admitted. 'I like to think it's one of my strengths.'

She rolled her eyes and made a move as if to leave, but he stayed where he was.

'Don't,' he murmured, feeling the subtle tension in her body. 'Stay here.'

She let out a breath. 'Why?'

'Because I have a proposition for you.'

'Isn't it a little late for a proposition?' The tension was still there, but he could feel her muscles starting to relax.

'Zoe,' he said quietly, holding her gaze. She had to know that he was serious about this, because the more he thought about it, the more he wanted it to happen, and she had to know that. 'I think we should keep doing this.'

'Doing what?'

'Having sex.'

Colour was beginning to deepen in her cheeks again, and with the sparkle of her silver eyes, he'd never seen anything so lovely.

'Why do you want to keep having sex?'

'Isn't it obvious?' He gave a subtle shift of his hips, pressing his rapidly hardening cock against her. 'Because I don't think that once is enough.'

She swallowed, the pulse at the base of her throat racing. 'This is the second time, if you recall.'

'Star,' he said. This was too important to him, and the little sarcastic comments were her way of distancing him, and he didn't want any distance, not now. 'I spent all day yesterday trying to resist you, and I couldn't. And today I fully expected to get in my jet and leave, but… You turned up in that fucking bikini and I couldn't think of anything else but you.'

She searched his face for a moment, as if she was looking for the truth. As if even now, even after what they'd just done together, she was still unsure of him. So he let her see that he meant it, and more, that he still felt it.

Abruptly, her lashes came down, veiling her gaze. She lifted a finger and drew a little circle with it on his shoulder. 'I just wanted to…torture you a bit,' she said at last. 'Because you walked away last night and—'

'I shouldn't have,' he interrupted, because the time for lies and excuses was over. 'I was trying to put some distance between us, because you were too great a temptation.'

Slowly her lashes lifted. 'I don't regret it,' she said starkly. 'Just so you know, I don't regret last night at all.'

'Neither do I.' He stared down at her. 'Which is why I think we should keep doing this. It's good, Zoe. Better than I've had with any other woman ever.'

Her lashes fluttered, shock crossing her face. 'Better?'

'Yes.' Again, she deserved the truth. 'So this is my proposition. I will be travelling for the next few weeks, and I want you to come with me.'

'Come with you?' Her eyes had gone wide. 'What do you mean?'

'You always wanted to travel, Star. Don't you remember? And I have offices and meetings I have to attend in the States, Japan and China, so why not come with me? You can do your own thing wherever we go, I won't stop you. I'll be working anyway.' He pushed a lock of hair back from her forehead. 'We have to live together for a year, if you remember, and we're married, so why not actually be husband and wife?'

She blinked again, her expression still one of surprise. 'But… I was going to stay here.'

'You didn't really want to be here anyway,' he reminded her, not above using a little emotional blackmail. 'Remember?'

She looked down at her finger still tracing circles on his skin. Her light touch was sending shivers through him, and it wasn't going to be long before his patience with it would be at an end.

'I know, but I don't think that being dragged around the world is great either.'

He gripped her chin gently, raising her gaze to his. 'Dragged? Really? Is that how you'd feel?'

The familiar spark of her temper flared briefly. 'All of this has been your choice, Archimedes. Not mine.'

He firmed his grip, because things were getting murky now and he couldn't have that. 'So this? Us together right now, that wasn't your choice?'

A soft breath escaped her. 'Okay, yes. Apart from this.'

A small knot of tension that had tightened inside him abruptly unravelled.

'This isn't an order,' he said. 'It's a request. I would like you to come with me, but if you don't, I won't force you.'

'Gee, thanks.'

'Zoe,' he said flatly, and her gaze came to his again. 'I mean it. I want you to come, make no mistake. But it will be your choice.'

She stared at him for a moment then sighed. 'So what exactly will I be doing while you're working? Playing the little woman at home?'

He snorted, letting go of her chin. 'As if you'd ever do that.'

'You know what I mean.'

'You can do whatever you want. Work, sightsee, read, whatever you want. But at night you'll be in my bed and in my arms.'

Her gaze narrowed. 'So essentially I'll be your unpaid escort.'

Archimedes's temper shifted, his patience fraying. 'Stop doing this, Zoe. Stop swiping at me. That's not what I said, and you know it. If you don't want to come, just say so.'

She turned her head away at that, looking out at the ocean, the lines of her face tight, and again he felt that unfamiliar regret twist inside him. He was tired of her hostility and he was tired of reacting to it, too. This, lying together here all tangled up, was so good. It felt right, and he wanted it.

'I'm sorry,' she said abruptly, her gaze still on the ocean. 'I guess I was just hoping for…more.'

'More? More of what?'

She kept her head turned away for a moment longer, then she turned back, her grey eyes full of a sudden determination. 'I don't want this to be only about sex, Archimedes. I want to know why you left. I want to know where you went. And I want to know why you're really agreeing to do this for Banks, including having a child for him.'

No one ever gets anything for free, remember?

Oh, he remembered. Everything came with a price, though why this price should feel so dangerous, he had no idea. All it meant was answering a few questions, nothing more than that. Yet something inside him was telling him that he had to be careful, that a few questions might lead to something else, though what else, he didn't know.

Still, in return for this? For having her soft, curvy body against his and her hunger his to feed? It seemed a decent trade.

'Okay,' he said. 'I can do that.'

'You wanted dinner every night,' she said, 'and I see no reason why we couldn't keep doing that wherever we are.'

Oh, fuck. The dinner. He'd forgotten entirely about his insistence on dinner. Well, he could hardly back down about that now. Besides, would it be so bad having dinner with her every night? He had his own curiosity about her too.

'Yes,' he acknowledged. 'We can keep doing that too.'

'Great, and I—'

'But I have functions to go to as well, and I think I'm going to insist on you accompanying me to all of them.' He wasn't going to let her drive all the bargains. He had a few of his own, apart from sex. 'And you'll wear whichever gown I decide on.'

Her dark brows drew down. 'Functions? Really?'

'Yes, functions. I want a trophy wife on my arm and you more than fit the bill.'

She scowled. 'I don't like parties.'

He smiled back. 'I don't care.'

A sigh escaped her. 'Okay, fine. But I'm terrible with

people so it'll be your own fault if I accidentally make your company stocks plunge in value.'

An odd feeling wound through him then, something that he normally only permitted to feel when it came to hacking particularly challenging online defences. Excitement, and along with it, anticipation. In fact, he couldn't remember the last time he'd felt either of those things, especially since he didn't do much hands-on hacking these days.

Dangerous to feel that. Especially about her.

Archimedes ignored the thought. After all, where exactly was this danger? Anticipating sex was hardly dangerous, not in the way he thought of it, and as for the dinners and functions, well, he enjoyed spending time with an intelligent and quick-witted woman. So why not feel some excitement about it? God knew there was little to feel excited about in his life currently.

'You will not cause my stocks to plunge,' he said. 'And even if you do, I'll siphon the money right back into my accounts again.'

Zoe frowned, then hit him on the arm. 'No, you will not,' she said sternly.

And another feeling joined the anticipation and the excitement. Gladness. This was familiar, him teasing her and her teasing him right back. This was what he remembered, the playfulness they'd once shared, and it hit him all of a sudden that he'd missed it.

You've missed her.

But that really was a dangerous thought, so he ignored it. Instead, he bent his head and kissed her again.

* * *

Zoe packed her duffel bag once again, stuffing back into it the few clothes she'd brought with her, trying to ignore the nagging feeling in her gut that somewhere, somehow, she'd made a mistake.

Perhaps she shouldn't have agreed to go with him so easily. Perhaps she shouldn't have agreed to go with him at all. Perhaps she should have chosen to stay here, on the island instead, where she wasn't around him twenty-four-seven.

But it was too late now. He'd offered her a choice—and yes, he'd made it very clear that it was *her* choice—and she'd taken it. Even though she knew there was danger there, a danger she couldn't pretend she didn't see coming.

Yet that was another thing that was too late. She knew what it was like to be in his arms, to have his mouth on her, to have him inside her. To taste him and have him taste her, and now she'd had it, she didn't think she could do without it. She'd planned on torturing him, holding out on him to make him absolutely desperate, yet in the end, she'd been the one who was desperate.

You're not the only one though, remember.

Yes, there was that at least. She'd pushed him to the edge in the pool and it had been so satisfying to watch him break, and then to break along with him. After that, how could she *not* accept his offer? To be in his bed every night and in his arms sounded like heaven. She wanted it too much, that was the issue, and that was the danger. Then she'd heaped yet more danger onto it, by insisting on dinner every night. Still, while she rather enjoyed being his sex object—she'd never been one before after all—she didn't want to be *only* that. She had questions to ask him and years to catch up on.

His insisting on functions and gowns had been annoying, but she hadn't been as outraged as she'd thought she would. No, she even rather liked the idea of being on his arm, wearing a gown that would make him desperate. Who was to say she couldn't still torture him a little?

He was right, too, she'd always wanted to travel, to see the world, and what better way to do that than on a billionaire's private jet? Away finally from Banks and dreary London. Doing the things she'd always told herself she wanted to do.

Even now he's still challenging you to get out of your comfort zone.

Yes, but really, wasn't it time for her to start challenging him for a change? To do that, though, she had to determine what his comfort zone was and then how to push him out of it. A difficult thing for a man that she suspected had no boundaries.

Then again, he hadn't liked it when she'd insisted on dinner, despite him being the one who'd suggested it in the first place. Maybe there was something in that. Maybe dinner and talking *was* out of his comfort zone.

She kept turning that over in her head as she finished packing then was escorted out to Kythea's tiny airstrip. The stewardess showed her and Archimedes to their seats, and ten minutes later they were in the air.

He was sitting opposite once again, and was staring at her. 'Want to join the mile high club?' His gaze glittered with heat.

Zoe gave him a prim look, noting the restless energy that buzzed around him. He was sitting still enough, but she could tell he was controlling himself, that he had himself on a tight leash.

'Not today,' she said, despite the way his gaze made her want to say yes, because she honestly couldn't think of anything she'd like better. But she didn't want him expecting her to say yes to everything he suggested, and also, maybe denial would be another thing to push him out of his comfort zone.

He leaned his head on his hand, his elbow propped on the seat arm. 'Why not?'

'Because I said so.' She gave him a look. 'Every night, you said. And it's not night right now.'

'It's night somewhere in the world.' He looked at her as if he wanted to eat her alive, and, quite honestly, it was all she could do not to get out of her seat and show exactly how much she wanted to join the mile high club, but no. It would do him good to wait.

'It's also dinnertime somewhere in the world,' she said. 'Perhaps we could talk first.'

He shifted, obviously annoyed by this, but he didn't look away. 'I'm surprised you suggested that, considering you were the one who didn't want to talk.'

'I'm surprised you hesitated when I did suggest it, considering that was your idea to start with.'

He shifted yet again, straightening and folding his arms across his broad chest. 'You have an answer for everything, don't you, Star?'

Star...

A traitorous warmth filled her at the sound of her pet name. She could still hear the way he'd said it to her in the heat of passion, his voice rough with desire. It sounded now as if he'd said it unconsciously and that too added to the warmth sitting inside her.

'I have to,' she said calmly, 'when dealing with you.'

Unexpectedly, he laughed, and she couldn't stop herself from smiling in return. It always made her feel as if she'd won a lottery whenever she made him laugh.

'That is true.' He gave her an abruptly serious look. 'Why did you never leave?'

The question came out of nowhere, in one of his lightning-quick changes of subject, and for a moment she could do nothing but blink at him, trying to process what he'd said.

'What? Leave who?'

'Banks.'

Instinctively, she felt defensiveness rise up inside her. 'It was my choice.'

'Was it?' Archimedes tilted his head, his sharp gaze reading every thought in her head.

'What happened to you?' she countered, because she didn't want to talk about why she hadn't left Banks, it would reveal too much about herself, about how needy she was, and she didn't feel ready to do that yet. Besides, this was supposed to be about putting *him* out of his comfort zone, not her. 'After you left,' she prompted. 'Where did you go? What happened to you?'

His eyes narrowed, obviously deciding whether to let her have the subject change or to push his question.

Then he leaned forward, his elbows on his knees, his fingers loosely laced together. 'You have to give me something, Zoe,' he said quietly, his gaze direct. 'Otherwise, our dinners together will be silent ones.'

She glanced away at that, her sense of vulnerability increasing. Because of course he was right. Her default for the past fifteen years, though, was to be wary. To keep her secrets, play her cards close to her chest, to protect herself. Because she'd been hurt and badly, first by the loss of her parents and then by the loss of him. Banks hadn't helped things either, using the things she loved against her to keep her at his side. So it was better to not give anything away, to armour herself against those who had the power to hurt her.

'I don't see you giving anything away,' she said, staring out of the window.

'No? Did you miss me telling you what Banks had on me? That's not something I tell anyone. In fact, no one knows except Banks and now, you.'

He did, unfortunately, have a point. He'd offered her that information last night over dinner, and it had shocked her that he'd been so honest. Now she felt guilty that she hadn't offered a piece of herself to him.

She let out a breath and turned back to meet his gaze. 'You left. And you never came back for me, never even contacted me apart from that job offer. So tell me, why do you deserve me giving you anything at all?'

He stared back. 'It mattered, didn't it? Me leaving.'

Of course he'd cut through all her defences like that, with one simple statement. The way he'd said it last night and she'd deflected and changed the subject. But did he really need her to acknowledge it? Could he not figure it out on his own?

'Why do you need me to tell you?' she asked.

'Because I want to hear it from you. I want to know.'

She let out a breath. Maybe it was her turn to give him something. Not everything. Just a little piece of honesty.

'Yes,' she said bluntly. 'It mattered. It mattered a lot.'

There was no satisfaction on his face as she expected, as if he'd scored a point. His features tightened instead, as if she was the one who'd hurt him.

'I'm sorry,' he said after a moment. 'I really am.'

He meant it, she knew. There was nothing but truth in his gaze. He really *was* sorry, and for some reason, her eyes filled and she had to turn away to the window again to hide them. She didn't want him to see just *how* much that mattered to her.

This is dangerous. All *of this is dangerous.*

Being with him was dangerous. Even talking to him was dangerous, especially when she knew now just how weak she was when it came to him. How he could get under her own guards and firewalls, like a virus infecting everything. Changing everything. Deleting her, rewriting her.

It scared her. It had taken her a long time to get over his loss and she didn't want to feel that way about him again, particularly when, after the year was over, they'd separate. This was only a temporary thing, even if it only lasted a year. And then there was having a baby to consider…

But beneath her fear lay something else. A strength

she hadn't been aware she'd had, and an excitement she couldn't deny.

It didn't matter the danger, she wanted this. She wanted him. And if she only had a year, maybe that was a good thing. Maybe she could throw herself into this thing they had, and leave the future to look after itself. After all, she had a plan, too, to push and challenge him, and she could hardly do that if she shied away from it herself.

If you wanted to drag someone through the fire, you had to go first.

So she didn't turn away She looked at him, deep into his eyes. 'Thank you,' she said, meaning it.

He must have seen her own truth, because he smiled suddenly like the sun coming out, and another wave of warmth hit her, making her heart ache.

'So,' she said quickly, ignoring the heat in her cheeks. 'You didn't even tell me where in the States we're going.'

'New York.'

Zoe grinned and allowed herself to feel just the tiniest bit excited. 'Oh, cool. I'd love to see MoMA.'

Archimedes's smile deepened. 'How about I take you?'

CHAPTER NINE

IT WAS CURIOUS how much Archimedes looked forward to finishing up his meeting so he could get back to Zoe. Normally, he was the last to leave, bringing work home with him wherever he went, losing himself in whatever project he had on at the time, always needing to get back and getting restless when he wasn't able to. But not this time.

He had a penthouse in Manhattan that overlooked Central Park, and he liked Zoe's round-eyed awe when she first walked into it. Not so much the fact that she was awed as her honest and unhidden reaction. The Zoe he remembered, not the guarded, wary woman she was now.

They had dinner that first night, as she'd insisted, though they talked mostly about what she wanted to see in New York rather than anything else. Afterwards, he took her to bed, because the flight had been a test of both his control and his patience, and he was tired of holding back.

Over the next couple of days Zoe was happy to sightsee while he worked, but he found himself growing more and more impatient with having to do that, wanting to be with Zoe instead, to show her the sights they'd talked about as kids. Coney Island. The Statue of Liberty. The Empire State Building and Rockefeller Center.

He knew he shouldn't be jealous that she didn't wait for him to do these things, but he was jealous all the same. And frustrated with himself. The work he was doing with Ares was important, and he shouldn't be getting distracted with a woman. Then again, she wasn't just any woman. She was Zoe and he hadn't seen her for years, and while in bed she was passionate, hungry and responsive, he found that that wasn't enough. He wanted more.

Five days after they'd arrived in New York, he came home from a meeting to find Zoe in the penthouse's huge living area, sitting on one of the soft sectional sofas, surrounded by souvenirs. There were pens, tea towels, postcards and fridge magnets, and it was obvious that she'd been to MoMA.

A pulse of irrational fury went through him at the sight, because he'd offered to take her himself. He'd *wanted* to take her himself and she hadn't told him she was going or waited for him either.

She looked up as he came into the room, her instinctive smile fading as she saw the look on his face. He'd come to love that smile of hers, it reminded him of themselves as kids, when she'd always look for him in every room she walked into, giving him her warm, bright, automatic Zoe smile. She'd begun doing that over the past couple of days, and he hadn't known how badly he'd missed it until he saw the lack of it right now. It only made his temper worse.

He should have said something self-deprecating and casual—at least he meant to. But what came out was, 'You went without me.'

Zoe blinked at his tone, then frowned. 'Went without you where?'

'To MoMA.' It shouldn't have sounded like an accusation, but it did.

'Oh.' She looked surprised. 'I didn't know you were so invested in it.'

He felt ridiculous all of a sudden, standing there being incensed that she'd gone somewhere without him. In fact, it shouldn't matter at all, because what did he care? It was just a fucking art museum. Except he couldn't shake his anger. He'd been looking forward to it, anticipating it, had even been planning a picnic in the park afterwards, and yet…

'I told you I wanted to take you,' he said, his voice coming out much sharper than it should. 'That's what I said in the plane, remember?'

Zoe's frown deepened into a scowl. 'If you'd wanted so badly to take me then you should have made arrangements and told me. I wanted to see it today so I went.'

Archimedes tried to keep hold of his temper. It wasn't good that he was so on edge, that his feelings were too close to the surface. Losing his temper because he felt left out of a trip was ridiculous.

You're getting too hung up on her. You need to put some distance between you.

He definitely should. This anger was verging into dangerous territory and he couldn't allow it. Yes, he'd asked her to come with him, to travel with him, and at night, when she was naked and in his arms, he'd never regretted asking her. But now…perhaps it hadn't been such a good idea after all.

What about Chloe? Perhaps you should make time to see her, forget Zoe for a while.

Oh, he remembered Chloe, his New York lover. Sensual and hungry, with a hot mouth. He'd had some good times with her. Pity the idea of her didn't excite him.

Zoe was getting up off the couch and coming towards him, still frowning. Her hair was loose down her back and she was wearing her usual T-shirt and jeans, nothing out of the ordinary. Except he felt suddenly desperate for her in a way that seemed almost uncontrollable.

'Why are you so angry?' she asked, coming to stand in front of him. 'I know you said you'd take me, but I didn't realise it was so important to you.'

'It's not,' he said curtly, reaching for her, his palms on her hips as he pulled her against him. 'It's just been a long day.'

She lifted her hands and pressed them against his chest as if she'd been doing so for years, as if touching him was her right, and the hungry thing inside him growled, wanting more.

'No,' she said. 'It mattered to you.'

'It's fine,' he lied, fitting her more firmly against him. 'I can take you somewhere else. We'll be going to Tokyo in a few days anyway, and I can show you some of the temples.'

But her frown didn't lift. 'Why are you lying?'

'I'm not lying,' he growled, curving his hands over her rear and squeezing her gently. 'You should make it up to me right now.'

She eyed him. 'It's not night, Demon.'

She had been calling him that lately, Demon, as if they were still who they'd been to each other when they were kids, and every time she said it, the sound sent an electric shock through him. It had the same effect on him now, and he squeezed her again, pressing her against his rapidly hardening cock.

'I don't care,' he said. 'Let's pretend it's night now.' When he'd insisted on her being in his bed every night, he hadn't thought she'd hold him to the letter of it. There had been times when he'd wanted her during the day, or in the morning or the afternoon, but she'd insisted on only sleeping with him at night, in bed. At first, he'd been content to wait because it was good for his self-control, but now he wasn't content at all. He thought he had some boundaries when it came to her, and now it was obvious that he didn't.

'No,' she said insistently. 'Remember what I said about not being your paid escort?'

Every part of him tightened with anger and frustration. 'Why?' he demanded. 'Why does that matter? You want me, Zoe, I know you do.' And of course she did, he could see how the silver of her eyes had darkened, how her muscles had relaxed and how, even now, she was melting against him.

'There have to be some boundaries,' she said, a huskiness in her voice despite what she'd said. 'If I give you an inch, you'll take a mile and you know you would.'

He made another frustrated noise and released her abruptly, his groin aching at the loss of her warmth. 'I don't give a fuck about boundaries and I don't think you do either.'

'Maybe,' she said. 'But I don't want to get confused about what's happening here. We're married and we're sleeping together, Demon. This is beginning to look like a real marriage and it can't be, you know that.'

'Of course I know that,' he snapped. 'You think I don't? It's just sex, Zoe. It's not a big deal.'

An expression he couldn't read flickered over her face then.

'Actually,' she said quietly, 'sex *is* a big deal. At least it is for me.' She took a little breath, as if bracing herself. 'You were my first, Archimedes.'

A cold wave of shock hit him. 'What?' he asked blankly. 'What do you mean I was your first?'

'What do you think I mean? I've never slept with anyone else except you.'

Instantly he thought back to that night on the terrace. How he'd grabbed and kissed her. How he'd swept everything off the table and put her up on it. How he'd shoved her thighs apart and pushed into her, too desperate for any niceties. Hell, he'd even thought that she was inexperienced.

You took no care with her and then afterwards you walked away.

The cold seeped through him like snow sliding down the back of his neck, chilling him to the bone. He *had* been careless that night. He'd lost control of himself, obeyed only his hunger, hadn't thought of the consequences, and he'd hurt her. Maybe not physically, but emotionally.

It reminded him of that cold morning on the yacht, in the stateroom, when he'd found out about his father, and how he'd looked around and seen himself clearly for the first time in ten years. Realising that, far from being in control of himself, he was letting his appetites control him.

He'd thought those appetites had been mastered, that sleeping with her would make things easier, but it hadn't. He was even more on edge than he had been in Greece, and that couldn't be allowed.

She must have seen the expression on his face because she said suddenly, 'You weren't to know. I didn't tell you.'

'Why didn't you?' he demanded, his whole body tense with shock.

If she was offended by his tone she didn't show it. 'Because it happened too fast and I was…'

She faltered, her mouth tightening, and he found himself staring at her, desperate to know what she'd been going to say, because she was right. This *did* matter. He'd been telling himself that sleeping with her was no big deal, but he'd assumed that she'd felt the same way. He'd assumed that, sure she might be inexperienced, but she'd slept with at least someone.

But she hadn't. She'd told him the truth. And what

was worse was that beneath the shock, something else shifted inside him, something possessive and jealous that was pleased he'd been her first. Pleased that she hadn't been with anyone but him.

'What?' he prompted, shoving that feeling away. 'You were what?'

Her lashes came down, her hands curling into fists. Protecting herself, he suddenly knew. She was protecting herself, and from him.

Are you surprised? You left her, and then you married her because you had to. Took her because you wanted to then dragged her here because you couldn't bear the thought of not having her in your bed. You haven't given one single shit about her feelings, so why wouldn't she protect herself?

'Zoe,' he said, not knowing what to say or what to offer her. Regret wasn't an emotion he allowed himself, not these days, but he could feel it inside him, sharp edges like razors, 'I shouldn't have done that. I'm—'

'I wanted you,' she said, ignoring him, her lashes coming up, revealing her gaze. 'I had a giant crush on you from the time I was eleven, even though I knew I was too young for you, and when you kissed me on the terrace that night, you made all my fantasies come true.'

Zoe had no idea why she was revealing this deeply held secret of hers and to the one man she should never reveal anything to, but…

He'd been so furious when he'd walked in and realised she'd gone to MoMA without him. Genuinely furious, and that had surprised her. She'd thought his offer in the plane had been a casual one, and she'd been impatient to go.

She'd loved being in New York—more than she'd thought she would—and had been feeling brave at going out and about herself, navigating her way through the busy city streets and riding the subway. She'd found herself on the street where MoMA was and thought she might as well go in.

She'd loved it, buying herself some ridiculous souvenirs including a silly fridge magnet for him, and she'd just been sorting through her spoils when he'd stalked in. He was all kinds of beautiful in his handmade blue suit and his white shirt with a scarlet silk tie, and she'd been about to leap to her feet and present him with the fridge magnet when he'd made it very clear that he was furious that she'd gone without him.

First she'd been surprised, then she'd felt guilty. She'd wanted to apologise, but then he'd grabbed her, his hands on her and his body pressed to hers, making her instantly ravenous. But she'd decided once they'd arrived in New York that yes, she'd be in his bed only at night. That she had to have some boundaries around him, mitigate the danger of him in some way. That way, she could have her cake and eat it too.

She hadn't meant to tell him she'd been a virgin but he'd been so ridiculously sulky about being denied, and his telling her sex was no big deal when it certainly was to her had been the last straw. So she'd told him straight out and his expression of genuine shock had caught at her heart.

It was an embarrassing thing to admit, and even more embarrassing to admit that she'd had a crush on him for so long, that he'd been in her fantasies for so long too, but the words had just…fallen out of her mouth. And now it was too late to call them back.

A heavy silence had fallen.

Archimedes's blue gaze held hers, shock still echoing in it.

She felt the urge to soften what she'd said, not make it sound quite so intense and desperate, but something inside her wouldn't let her. She'd been hiding herself for a long time. Hiding her feelings, pretending that nothing mattered, that nothing was a big deal. But things were a big deal, sex with him was a big deal. Being with him full stop was a big deal, and she couldn't keep pretending any more.

He'd told her that she had to give him something and so she had. She'd given him everything, and while it felt dangerous, reckless, it also felt…good. Why shouldn't he know what he was to her? What he'd been? Why shouldn't he know that everything she did with him felt momentous and she couldn't act as if it wasn't?

'Your fantasies?' he demanded, as if she'd said something hurtful. 'Being shoved onto a table and screwed without any care was really one of your fantasies?'

Her throat tightened at the glitter of anger in his eyes, but she could hear the self-loathing in his voice. It wasn't directed at her.

'Yes,' she said simply. 'But only being screwed by you.'

To her shock, this time he abruptly turned away,

raking a hand through his black hair as he strode over to the windows, his back to her.

'Don't make this into something it's not,' he said after a moment, his voice flat. 'Sex might be a big deal to you, but it isn't to me.'

Something squeezed tight behind her breastbone, but she ignored it. He was lying, she was sure of it. If sex truly hadn't been a big deal to him then he wouldn't have been so shocked when she'd told him she was a virgin. He wouldn't now be turning away, his whole posture tense. Why was he lying though? Was it to protect her or himself?

'I don't think that's true,' she said, as the realisation hit her.

'It doesn't matter what you think.' He didn't turn.

She ignored that. 'Why are you lying, Archimedes?'

He was silent a moment, then turned abruptly, the expression on his face hard, blue eyes glittering like hard, cold sapphires. 'Once the year is up, that's all. I'll be gone, Zoe. You understand that, don't you?'

'Yes,' she said, both to herself and to him. 'What has that got to do with anything?'

'There will be no further relationship.' He took a step forward as if to emphasise the fact. 'It's not personal. I just don't do relationships with anyone.'

Something inside her clenched tight, but she dismissed it, concentrating on him instead. He was very, very certain about this, wasn't he?

'Yes, I get it,' she said. 'But you still haven't answered the question.'

He let out a breath and raked another restless hand

through his hair. 'You want to know what happened to me after I left? I went to work for the Russian mob. I stole for them, helped them take down their enemies, did every bad thing you could possibly imagine. And I didn't care. Because the only thing that mattered was having money and power. At first, it was all about coming back for you, Zoe. To be powerful enough to get you away from Banks.'

That was *not* what she'd expected him to say. She frowned and opened her mouth to speak, but he said, 'I haven't finished. Just…let me say it.'

Zoe closed her mouth and nodded.

'But then I forgot about you. I liked the power being with the Russians gave me. I liked the money. I liked the thrill of stealing and taking down our enemies and… I lost myself to it for a whole decade.' Shadows moved over his face. 'Then one day I decided to find my father, see where I came from, and that was…a mistake. I woke up on a billionaire's yacht after a party, hungover and with no memory, to an email in my inbox telling me that my father was in an Athens prison doing time for murder. He turned out to be just a violent thug.' Archimedes let out a breath. 'I thought I was in control of myself, of my life, but that morning I realised that I was in control of nothing and that I *was* him. And worse, I'd become someone you wouldn't have gone with even if I had come back for you. I had to get back on the right path, so that's what I did.'

It felt as if a giant fist had taken hold of her heart and was squeezing it, making it hurt. Hearing that he'd been intending to come back for her right from the beginning was a sweet kind of pain. And as to what he'd done in those years…it didn't shock her or disgust her. It only made her feel a desperate pity for him. She could see how such a life would appeal to a man like him, especially when he'd been so young, and that it would be so easy to get lost in it.

'Archimedes—' she began.

'That's why I never contacted you,' he said starkly, ignoring her. 'I was lost for ten years and then it took another five to get back on track. Also, I didn't want to bring you into it or drag you down with me.'

She took an instinctive step towards him, wanting to touch him, ease him, but he went on. 'I'm on edge, Zoe. Getting angry about you going to MoMA without me is an example of how just how on edge I am, and that's dangerous for me and it's dangerous for you.'

The fist around her heart squeezed again. 'How? You pulled yourself out of it. You left it behind, which some people never do.'

'I nearly didn't, though. That's the point. You're like a drug, Star. I want more and more, I can't get enough, and if I'm not careful, I'll fall back down that hole again, and this time I'll take you with me.'

Cold washed through her, the shadows in his eyes making her shiver, a terrible guilt creeping through her. The decision she'd made to torture him, push him, now seemed so very, very wrong. It was like waving a needle at a junkie.

'I'm sorry,' she said hoarsely. 'I think I made things worse when I—'

'You didn't know,' he interrupted. 'And you didn't

make things worse. I just overestimated my control around you.'

She swallowed, her chest feeling tight and sore. 'So, where does that leave us?'

He stared at her for a long moment, saying nothing. Then he crossed the distance between them, stopping in front of her and lifting his hands to cup her face between his palms.

'A year, Star. A year for us to get rid of this physical chemistry. But I can't do any more than that. You understand that, don't you?'

His hands were warm on her skin and he smelled familiar and so delicious it almost made her mouth water. It didn't matter how long this was for, it really didn't. She didn't want to be the cause of anything that might make things worse for him, and so if he only wanted a year, that was what he'd get.

You always knew being with him would be an impossibility.

The thought wound through her, sharp-edged and painful, but she ignored it.

'Yes,' she said, even though, deep down, there was a part of her that didn't. 'What about the baby thing?'

'What about it? That's something that still needs to happen.'

For a second she allowed herself to think about the child they'd promised Banks—*their* child—and she was conscious that the thought was a painful one. It seemed somehow more real now that they were sleeping together, and she was disturbed by how much her heart ached at the thought of giving that child away. But that was what Banks had demanded, and she needed the money he'd promised her. She had to follow through.

'So,' she said, 'are we going to employ a doctor for that?'

'Why?' His gaze suddenly became very focused. 'When you're in my bed every night.'

That thought too was a painful one, their child being conceived out of passion and pleasure, and the glory of being in his arms. She didn't want that. She couldn't give up a child who'd been conceived like that.

'No,' she said. 'We will still need a doctor for that.'

'Why?' He frowned. 'Wouldn't that be pointless?'

'I can't do it, Demon,' she said, her voice getting a little husky. 'I don't want to give up any child conceived in your bed. I *can't*.'

He was quiet a moment, giving her a searching look. Then his thumbs moved caressingly on her cheeks, stroking her skin.

'Okay,' he said. 'Then we'll do it the way we originally planned.'

She thought that might make her feel better, but it didn't.

'Just so you know,' she said, since he'd given her something of himself. 'Whatever you did after you left, whatever hole you fell into, I don't judge you. You made it out and that's what matters, not what happened while you were in it.'

Something in his deep blue gaze softened. Then he bent and brushed a kiss over her mouth.

She allowed herself to lean into him for a second. Then she remembered something. 'Oh,' she said a little breathlessly when he lifted his head, 'I got you a present.'

He lifted a brow in that sexy way he had. 'Oh?'

'It's a fridge magnet.'

A smile curved his mouth. 'How did you know? I really hope that's my wedding present.'

For the first time since she'd left London the ache in Zoe's heart eased at the sight of that smile. There was no point in dwelling on how quickly a year would pass. The only thing she could do was live it and let the future take care of itself.

CHAPTER TEN

ARCHIMEDES STOOD BY the wall in the crowded ballroom, watching the dancers in the middle of it, and one woman in particular. It was at some interminable tech fundraising gala in one of Shanghai's opulent towers and, as she'd promised him, Zoe had come along at his side. This was the third function she'd attended with him and, like the other two, she'd worn the dress he'd chosen for her. This one was like molten silver that poured over her body, clinging to every luscious curve, and he'd been delighted when she'd tried it on before the gala and clearly liked what she saw in the mirror. The pleasure she took in the dress made him feel pleased too, especially because he'd chosen it for her.

That pleasure was draining away now, however, because she'd been asked to dance by a Spanish duke, and now she was there on the floor, revolving in the arms of a handsome Spaniard, and all he wanted to do was to punch the guy in the face.

You're jealous.

He wished that wasn't true, that he didn't feel this anger seething in his heart, burning like a hot coal, but he did and he couldn't lie. It *was* jealousy. He'd thought he'd got past it after she went to MoMA without him, but no, apparently not. He didn't want her in anyone's arms but his, and the feeling was getting worse and worse, no matter how many times he told himself he was being ridiculous.

He'd thought that telling her what he'd done after he'd left Banks's house and what had happened to him, and why he had to be so careful around her, would have made things easier between them, yet it hadn't. Her response had been far more accepting than he'd expected and the way she'd looked up at him when he'd cupped her lovely face between his palms and told him that she didn't judge him, that the fact that he'd managed to pull himself out was the most important thing to her… Well, that had made his heart feel too big for his chest at the same time as it cut him to the bone.

He'd left her and never came back, and yet she had grace enough to accept his apology for that, as well as giving him understanding and compassion when he'd told her why he'd never come back for her. She was a better person than he was, a more giving, generous person.

He didn't like that she'd refused to allow them to conceive their child in his bed, that she still wanted a fertility doctor to handle it, but he understood her reasoning. She'd always had a bigger heart and a kinder soul than he ever had. God, she was a better person, full stop, while he stood here, burning with possessive jealousy.

Over the past few weeks he'd tried to moderate himself, to keep hold of his escalating emotions, but it had been far more difficult than he'd ever thought it would be. Their dinners hadn't touched on anything too personal, but she'd told him more about her plans for the company she intended on starting up. He'd loved the idea and told her so, because it was very her. Helping people, wanting to put her skills to better use than what Banks had taught them, was Zoe to a T.

She'd asked him about Ares in turn, and he'd waxed lyrical about it, telling her all about his plans for it in intimate detail, the way he did when he was enthusiastic about something, and she'd asked questions, made some good points, and then confessed she'd been testing his firewalls and had found a backdoor that one of his developers had missed. Only Zoe would have found a weakness in his programming and he loved that she'd spotted it. It made him feel proud, even though he knew he had no right to be.

And then after their dinners, when he took her to bed, their passion burned bright, getting hotter and hotter, as if fuelled by something more than mere physical desire.

So much for putting boundaries around their relationship.

Tokyo hadn't helped either. To stop his unreasonable feelings of jealousy, he'd decided to go sightseeing with her, showing her his favourite places—a noodle shop in Harajuku. A temple with the most beautiful garden. A warehouse with all the latest tech. She'd loved them just as much as he did, and her obvious pleasure made everything worse. He wanted more of her, more and more, as if proving to him that she was a drug he couldn't resist.

It was a problem and he didn't see any solution to it. Or rather, there were two solutions. One, he sent her back to Greece and away from him. Or two, he kept her. He kept her forever.

It should have been an easy choice. Sending her away would definitely be the best option, but he couldn't bear the thought of it. He couldn't bear coming back to whatever place they were living in and not having her in his bed waiting for him, or not even there at all. Sure, he could have another lover easily enough, but that didn't excite him. That didn't turn him on, not like she did.

Which meant the only other option—keeping her. Yet that wasn't any kind of solution either. Zoe wasn't a woman he could lock away in a glass case, or keep in a bank vault. She'd lost the only family she'd ever had twice, once when her parents had died and once when he'd left, and he knew she wanted one. That conversation about the baby back in New York was evidence enough of that.

Except he would never be able to give her the family she wanted. He wasn't made to have a family of his own, a wife and children, a contented life. He was too restless, too driven, and unable to stay in one place for too long. And his control over himself had to be absolute, it *had* to be, and how could he do that with a family? It was hard enough when it was just him alone.

It was just such a shitty dilemma. If he kept her, he'd deny her the chance of the family he knew damn well she longed for, because he was possessive and jealous, and he couldn't bear the thought of her finding happiness with someone else.

There's only one option then, isn't there?

He tensed, watching as the Spaniard's hand moved lower, to the small of Zoe's back. She was looking up at the man and smiling that precious Zoe smile, the one that should be for him and only him. And he was moving before he knew what he was doing, shoving himself away from the wall and heading straight towards her.

'I'm cutting in,' he growled at the Spaniard, almost shoving the man aside as he took Zoe in his arms. The man stared daggers at him but stepped back, which was just as well because Archimedes was in no mood to be disobeyed.

'What's wrong with you?' Zoe asked, glaring at him. 'I was enjoying talking to Julio.'

'I don't care.' He slid his own hand down to the small of her back, spreading his fingers out possessively, urging her closer, feeling the jealousy in him calm. 'You're my trophy wife, not his.'

She gave him a searching look. 'Please don't tell me you're jealous, Demon.'

Archimedes was in no mood to pretend either. 'And if I was?'

Her cheeks went pink. 'Why? You've got no reason to be.'

'You were smiling at him.'

'I was being polite.'

'I don't want you to be polite.'

Zoe rolled her eyes as they turned slowly around the room. 'I smile at you too, if you remember.'

His shoulders ached, tension crawling through them. Her body was warm against his, the scent of her driving him insane. He'd had her all night the night before, so he shouldn't be so hungry now, yet he was. He was beginning to think that he'd always be hungry for her, and he hated how he had no control over that.

'This can't go on,' he said abruptly.

Her eyes widened. 'What can't go on?'

'You. Me. Us.' He gripped her delicate fingers. 'I shouldn't want you the way I do, and I shouldn't be so fucking angry every time I see you with another man.'

She blinked, her mouth opening in surprise.

'There are only two solutions, Zoe,' he went on, because now the words were out of his mouth he might as well continue. 'Either you go back to Greece, the way we originally planned, or you're mine and mine completely until one or other of us decides it's over.'

Her gaze flickered and she shut her mouth. He couldn't tell what she was thinking and it frustrated him. It frustrated him that he even wanted to know but, as he was learning, she was the exception to every rule, and he couldn't make it otherwise.

'What do you mean, I'm yours and yours completely?' she asked carefully.

'We continue the way we're doing now, you being with me and in my bed every night. You remaining my wife.'

'But I'm already doing those things.' Her voice was

calm, and that rubbed against his already raw anger like a burr. It felt as if she was placating him.

'Don't try to manage me, Zoe,' he growled. 'It's not a joke.'

'I know that,' she said in the same calm tone, which only enraged him further.

He stopped in the middle of the dance floor and released her, only to keep a hold of her hand, then he turned and pulled her through the crowd and down a hallway, until he came to a deserted and shadowed alcove. Then he pushed her into it, caging her against the wall with his arms.

'I said it's not a joke.' His voice was low and rough, and he couldn't keep the demand from it.

Her gaze had gone wide, but as she looked up at him, a crease had appeared between her brows. She stared at him a moment before reaching up to cup his face, her palms cool against his hot skin. 'I'm not going anywhere, Demon,' she said softly. 'I'm not going to leave.'

Was that all he needed to know? He wasn't sure. All he knew was that the hunger inside him was screaming for her as if she was his new drug and he was desperate for a fix.

'You should go back to Greece,' he said, forcing out the words. 'You should get away from me.'

Her grey eyes were like summer rain, cooling the desperate heat inside him. 'I shouldn't do anything I don't want to do,' she said. 'And I don't want to leave you.'

He gripped her wrists, pulling her hands away so

he could press his mouth against each palm. 'It would be better for you if you did.'

'I don't see how.' She pulled her wrists from his grip, dropping her hands to his waist and pulling him against her. 'If you want me to be yours completely then I will be. I already am anyway.'

She was soft against him, feminine musk and delicate heat. His North Star.

'The family you want,' he said. 'You won't have it if you stay with me. You understand that?'

Shadows moved in her eyes before quickly vanishing, but not before he saw them. It made an iron band tighten around his chest.

'Yes,' she said. 'I understand.'

This will hurt her and you both know it.

It would, he was well aware. But he couldn't promise her something he couldn't actually deliver. It was best she knew now, before things got too intense between them.

A little late for that.

He ignored the thought, trying to calm himself, still the frantic circling of his brain. She'd agreed to stay with him and so there was nothing for him to worry about, nothing for him to be desperate about, and nothing to be jealous about. She was his and she'd told him she was.

'Demon,' she said softly, the silver glitter of her eyes dazzling him, 'I'm here for you.'

It was too much. He couldn't hold back any longer. Bending his head, he covered her mouth with his, wanting to taste the delicious flavour of her, to imprint himself so completely on her that she would never want anything or anyone else but him. She didn't hold back either, her lips parting beneath his, welcoming him with her own hunger, and he was lost.

He pushed her hard against the wall, already reaching to pull up her gown, and she didn't protest. Her own fingers were at his belt, undoing his buttons and then the zip of his trousers, as frantic as he was.

She gasped as he slid his hands up her thighs, taking the skirts of her gown with it, before sliding his fingers between her thighs. She was already wet and hot for him and she shuddered as he stroked her. Her head fell back as he slid his hands to cup her rear, lifting her against the wall, readying her, before pushing deep inside.

She groaned and he kissed her, muffling her sounds with his mouth in a hot, desperate kiss. They were in public, where anyone could see them, but he didn't care and it was plain that she didn't either. So he didn't stop. He moved, pushing deeper, harder, and her teeth sank into his bottom lip in reaction, which made him do it again and again.

This was how it should always be between them. Desperate, feverish. Hungry. The two of them joined together in pleasure, with him deep inside her, as close as he could be to her. This was how his brain calmed, how he could find peace, only with her.

This time he was good, he stroked her clit just the way she liked it as he moved, making sure to give her as much pleasure as she was giving him. Then he eased the strap of her gown off one shoulder so one breast was bare for him to tease with his fingers. She arched against the wall, another soft sound escaping her, and by now he knew her body. He knew when she was almost there and so he drew it out, showing her how good he could make her feel. Showing her that there was nothing better than them together like this and that she didn't need anything more than this.

Then, when he was ready, he stroked her one last time, burying himself deep inside her, covering her mouth and stemming her cry of release, before turning his face into her neck and letting the orgasm swallow him whole.

Zoe slumped against Archimedes, her body held upright by his, shaking and shivering with the aftershocks of pleasure. She could feel his warm breath against her skin, the tension that had been gripping him so tight now gone.

She had no idea what had gone wrong out in the ballroom, but something had, and she didn't think it was just because she'd been dancing with the Spanish duke.

They hadn't been in Shanghai long, but she'd been looking forward to doing a bit of sightseeing with him. She'd loved him taking her around Tokyo and showing her all his favourite haunts, especially because she knew they'd become her favourites as well.

Yet she could tell he was finding things between them difficult. It was subtle, tension in his body, the way he looked at her, the way he touched her. As if he was at war with himself. Resisting her, that was what he was doing—or at least trying to resist her. She'd wanted to talk more about it at their dinners together, but she didn't want to rock the boat, especially when their pleasure at night was so intense.

So she hadn't protested when he'd kept her close all night through, firmly at his side, and she'd only said yes to the duke because Archimedes had been talking with some colleagues.

Fury had blazed in his eyes when he'd cut in, his hands on her firm and possessive. He was jealous, she could see that, but there was something more to it, something desperate. She wanted to calm him, soothe him, ease whatever pain he was in, so of course she'd agreed to his demand that she be his.

There had been a slight waver in her resolve when he'd stated that he couldn't allow her to have a family with him but what else could she say? She either chose that or she chose someone else. She couldn't choose both. The thought of giving him up for a family that didn't even exist yet wasn't a sacrifice she could make, and so it had to be him. You couldn't have something for nothing, wasn't that the lesson Banks had taught them?

She stroked his black hair, letting him rest against her for a long moment and a silence fell between them. It didn't matter that they'd just had sex in a public place. The Zoe she'd been before she'd married him would have been appalled, but the Zoe she was now didn't care. Having him was all she wanted.

Slowly, before she was ready, he lifted his head and began dealing with his clothing and then hers with careful hands. And that was when it hit her, like ice water down the back of her neck.

'We didn't use protection,' she said, her voice shaky.

His gaze met hers, shock darkening the blue. He let out a breath, raking his fingers through his black hair. 'I…didn't think,' he murmured.

'I should have said something.' Panic was beginning to set in, her heartbeat accelerating, because this could mean pregnancy. This could mean her being pregnant with his child, a child conceived in desperation and hunger, and then having to give that up…

'I can't get pregnant,' she said. 'I can't.'

Archimedes looked down at her silently, his face unreadable. He didn't want this either, he'd already told her that, and now his desperation and hers had complicated an already complicated situation.

'I need to see the doctor,' she went on when he didn't say anything. 'Get something—'

But he silenced her with a finger across her lips, a familiar anger burning in his eyes. Except it wasn't directed at her, just like it hadn't been directed at her out on the dance floor. It was an anger directed elsewhere.

'No,' he said flatly. 'No doctor.'

She pulled his finger away. 'If I'm pregnant—'

'If you're pregnant, then you will have the baby,' he finished as if that was a foregone conclusion.

Zoe stared up at him. 'I told you in New York that I didn't want to get pregnant like this. I don't…want to give up a baby—our baby—to Banks.'

'Then we won't,' he said as if that, too, was a foregone conclusion.

Shock wound through her. 'But you don't want children, Demon. You told me that. You were quite happy to give our child up to Banks.'

His gaze was cool and very, very certain, as if he'd come to some decision. 'I didn't want children, no,' he said. 'And yes, I was happy for Banks to bring any child of ours up. But I've changed my mind. If you're pregnant then we're keeping the baby, no argument.'

Her shock deepened. 'He's blackmailing you. And that's not even mentioning the money he was going to pay me.'

'I'm not giving our child up.' The look in his eyes burned. 'If you need money for your company, I'll help you.'

Her throat closed, a shaky feeling gripping her, unexpected tears filling her eyes. 'I don't want to give it up either, that's not what I'm saying. I don't care about the money. But I do care about you going to jail.'

All at once the burning coals in his gaze cooled and he lifted a hand to her cheek, cupping it in a way that made her heart ache.

'That's not going to happen,' he said, his voice full of conviction. 'I'll find a way around it. But what's done is done, and if you are indeed pregnant, I'll make sure no one takes the child from us, understand? I didn't want children, but if a child comes from this then I will take responsibility for them, Star. Don't worry.'

The words should have reassured her, but she didn't feel reassured. She felt afraid for reasons she couldn't articulate. 'Take responsibility' sounded so cold. Then again, he'd been very clear that what was between them was only sex, nothing more. This was something neither of them had anticipated.

'What will we tell Banks?' she asked.

'Nothing. It'll take a couple of weeks for us to know for sure if you're pregnant anyway, and he specified a year of us living together. We have some time to solve the problem.'

It came to her then, like a ton of bricks descending on her shoulders, what exactly she'd agreed to when she'd told him she was his. She would have to live with him the way they were doing right now, have to be around him every day, be in his bed every night. And what would happen if she was indeed pregnant? What would their relationship be like? Would he want more children? What kind of family would they have? This wasn't his choice and she didn't like thinking about what that would mean for them in the long run.

You know what it means.

Yes, she had a horrible feeling she did. What would hold them together? What would be the glue that made them a family? It wasn't only a child, it was more than that. It was love. What she'd once had as a child, and then never again.

Zoe's mouth dried and abruptly she didn't want to be standing there any more, not with him so close. His physical nearness only seemed to highlight what she was beginning to realise was a great emotional distance. He viewed his emotions as something to fight and resist, while she gave herself up to hers. Her anger, her loyalty, her love…

You love him.

Awareness caught her by the throat, insistent, demanding. Oh, she'd loved him years ago, when they were children together, but that had been a sibling kind of love. When she'd got older, it had morphed into something more, only to have that shatter when he'd left. But of course that was why she'd been so hurt, and why she'd held onto her anger for so long.

She loved him. She always had.

Desperate to get away, so he wouldn't see what was in her eyes, she made to move past him, but his hand shot out, trapping her against the wall again.

'What is it?' he asked, frowning down at her in concern. 'You're upset. Is it just the thought of pregnancy?'

Her pulse thudded in her ears. He could never know, she knew that already. She could never tell him. '"Just" the pregnancy?' she said instead. 'There's no just about it, Archimedes. I wanted children. I wanted a family. I wanted what I lost when my parents died, but that's not what you're offering, is it?'

A muscle pulsed in his strong jaw. 'I can give you some of those things,' he said after a moment. 'Not all, but some.'

'I don't just want one child.' There was no point hiding how she felt about a family, at least. 'I want more. I want them to have the childhood neither of us did.'

His blue gaze flickered then steadied. 'If you want more, then we can have more. And they will have the best childhood we can give them.'

She shouldn't say it, she shouldn't. And yet she couldn't help herself. 'And love?' she asked. 'What about that?'

There was no flickering in his gaze now. It was steady. 'You may not be pregnant,' he said, ignoring the question. 'In which case this will all be a moot point.'

It was true. There was no guarantee that anything would come from this, and really, it would be better for both of them if nothing did. But deep in her heart, she did want something to come from it. She wanted a child, *his* child.

Except there was no point in thinking about that now. What would happen would happen and she had no choice about it, so why keep torturing herself? Tonight she was in Shanghai and she had him, and that was all she wanted. Even if her heart disagreed.

'True,' she made herself say. 'Would you like another dance?'

The expression on his face eased. 'I thought you'd never ask.'

Zoe pasted a smile on her face and let him lead her back to the ballroom. If this was all she'd ever have, then she would take it. But there was always tomorrow. Tomorrow, after all, was another day.

CHAPTER ELEVEN

SIX WEEKS AFTER Shanghai and in Italy for a meeting, Archimedes came back to his Roman residence—a palazzo just outside the city—to find Zoe sitting cross-legged on the sofa, her attention on her laptop.

As always, it gave him immense satisfaction to see her in any of his houses, because she always looked as if she belonged there, as if this was her home as much as it was his.

Things between them had been better after Shanghai. Since she'd agreed to stay with him, the burning in his heart had eased, and he was able to stay on top of his possessiveness and jealousy. He still berated himself for his slip in forgetting the condom, but he found he wasn't as upset about it as he'd thought.

A certain fatalism had gripped him in that moment, because it had happened and nothing could change that, regardless of what he wanted. But it had been Zoe's response that had truly affected him. She'd looked up at him with fear in her eyes, reminding him of the contract they'd signed with Banks, and the ramifications of having to give their child up. He'd thought he'd still be fine at the thought of having Banks bring up their son or daughter, that all he'd need to do to ease her fear was to say a few soothing words, give her a few kisses.

But he wasn't fine and he knew she needed more than that. She deserved more than that. So he'd told her that if she was pregnant, they'd find a way around Banks's demands. That he would take care of her and the baby, and he meant it. He wouldn't leave her alone, *couldn't* leave her alone, not now.

Of course, then she'd had to go and mention love, and since he couldn't bring himself to lie to her, he'd ignored her question instead. She hadn't brought up his lack of answer since, so he'd let it lie. His answer wouldn't change anyway. Love was not something he could afford to indulge in even if he wanted to.

Archimedes walked down the long, light salon that ran down one side of the palazzo and sat in the armchair opposite Zoe on the sofa, watching her fingers fly across the keys.

'Hi, honey, I'm home,' he said.

'Clearly.' She didn't look up.

He leaned his elbow on the arm of the chair and rested his head in his hand. 'What are you doing?'

'I keep finding flaws in your supposedly impregnable firewall.'

He laughed, unable to help himself. 'More? I really need to talk to my developers.'

'You should.' She hit a few more keys. 'They've been kind of lazy.'

'You really should be working for me,' he said. 'I could use you.'

'No, thanks. I'm going to set up my own company, remember?'

Oh, he remembered. He was still a little jealous of her idea.

'Why didn't you ever do that sooner?' he asked without thinking. 'You can't tell me Banks didn't pay you enough. Or did he do something to make you stay?'

Her fingers paused on the keyboard. 'I felt sorry for him,' she said after a moment. 'He's alone, with no family or friends, and he's the only father figure I ever had. I couldn't leave him.'

A familiar, tight feeling ached behind his ribs. She was so very loyal, giving that loyalty freely even when the person she'd given it to didn't deserve it.

'I don't understand,' he said. 'He ran his own mini crime empire for years, using kids as his foot soldiers, and then he told you that I'd just left without saying goodbye. That kind of man doesn't deserve anyone's loyalty.'

'Who appointed you the judge of what people deserve?' she asked, a sudden sharp edge in her voice. 'We're all flawed, Demon. We all have our weaknesses, just as we all have our strengths. Anyway, Banks left behind the black hat stuff years ago. He's been hiring out his services and mine as online security consultants.'

Archimedes shifted in his chair, restless again in a way he hadn't been for weeks.

You don't like that she's right. Especially since you've been trying to overcome your flaws for years.

He shifted yet again, not liking that thought either.

He hadn't been 'trying'. He'd done it. He'd overcome his many, many weaknesses and while he'd had a few issues with Zoe, he didn't think they would persist. Not now she was his permanently.

'I see,' he said. 'What changed his mind?'

'I did.' She looked back down at her keyboard. 'I told him I *would* leave if he didn't stop stealing from people. So he did.'

Archimedes stared at her lovely face, her silky black eyelashes veiling her gaze.

'He must have loved you,' he said. 'There's no other reason he'd give that up.'

'No,' she said. 'He just loved my skills.'

Something stilled inside him, caught by the faintest echo of pain in her voice. 'What makes you say that?' he asked.

She didn't stop typing, nor did she look at him. 'I mean, what else would he have loved?'

A little shock went through him, a small bright arrow of pain. Did she really think that about herself? That her hacking skills were all there was to her?

You know that's what she thinks. She's been left and abandoned by everyone she loves.

Oh, he was well aware. And it explained why she'd stayed, because she wouldn't want to do to anyone else what had been done to her.

The pain inside him deepened. It made him angry that she had so little regard for herself when she was intelligent, loyal, generous and funny.

'I can think of a few things,' he said, again without thinking.

Her head came up and she met his gaze, and he could see hurt as clear as day in her eyes.

'Zoe?' He leaned forward in sudden concern. 'What's wrong?'

She looked away but not before he saw the telltale glint of tears in her eyes, and instantly every part of him tightened.

'What is it?' He shoved himself from the armchair and crossed the distance between them. 'What's happened?'

Her expression was tight. 'Don't say things you don't mean. Oh, and by the way, you'll be very pleased to know that I'm not pregnant after all.'

For a second he couldn't quite take in why she was talking about pregnancy when they'd been talking about her.

Time has been passing, remember?

Of course it had. But for the first time in his life, he'd tried not to be aware of it. Tried not to think about it. And now there was a hollow feeling inside him, as if the sun had gone behind a cloud and the room had darkened a little.

Madness. He couldn't have actually wanted her to be pregnant, could he?

You do. You know you do.

The thought wound through him as he stared down at her small figure, cross-legged and self-contained on the sofa, her gaze on her screen. Not looking at him. Very determinedly not looking at him. She'd wanted it, hadn't she? She'd wanted his child. And he did too. He couldn't run from the knowledge any more. He had to admit it to himself. He wanted their child and he wanted her.

A tear slipped down her cheek, and he couldn't stand it any more. He bent down and took the laptop away from her, before sitting down beside her on the sofa. Then he turned her face towards him, and yes, there were the tears and the disappointment.

'Zoe,' he murmured, stroking her cheek. 'Star, please…'

She remained sitting stiffly, tears slipping down her cheeks. Not hiding herself from him or hiding her feelings.

'I know you don't want kids, Archimedes. But I do.'

'Then let's have them,' he said, knowing the moment the words were out of his mouth that he couldn't say no to her, not about this. 'We could have one, two, as many as you like.'

She looked at him, not giving him the lovely Zoe smile he'd expected, not giving him anything at all. 'This was never your choice, Demon. You're only saying that because I'm disappointed, not because you actually want kids.'

'That's not true,' he said. 'I want your child. Our child.'

'But you wouldn't have wanted that if we'd used protection back in Shanghai, would you?'

He wished he could deny it, tell her she was wrong, but she wasn't. If they'd used protection he would never have even considered it.

'But we didn't use protection.' He stroked away a tear with his thumb. 'And it's my choice now.'

But she pulled away from him, looking down at her hands. 'You never answered my question back in Shanghai. When I asked you about love.'

Instantly he stiffened. 'What about it?'

Her gaze came back to his. 'Having children includes love, Archimedes. Having a family includes love.'

The hollow sensation in his stomach increased. He'd been hoping she'd forgotten about the question she'd asked him, but of course she hadn't.

'What are you asking?' A stupid question because he knew what she was asking. *Exactly* what she was asking.

'You have to love children,' she said. 'You have to.'

'Why?' Another stupid question. 'No one loved me.'

'That's a lie.' Somehow, her voice had become firmer, the look in her eyes steadier. 'I loved you, Archimedes.'

Of course she loved you. How did you not know?

Because no one else had ever loved him, so why should he know? His father had let him go and his mother had abandoned him. The only person who'd ever wanted him had been Banks and he'd always been clear that was only because of his skills.

But not Zoe. She'd loved him for who he was, loved the boy he'd once been. Except…he wasn't that boy now and he'd never be that boy again.

There was a pain in his heart, a deep, acute ache. Yes, he knew all too well what she was asking him, just as he knew what he was offering her was not what she wanted. And he couldn't give it—he couldn't. He didn't know what love felt like, but he knew that it was powerful, that it would end up controlling him if he let it. And he would let it, because that was what happened when he let his emotions get the better of him. He couldn't allow that, not even for children of his own.

What kind of father would you be? You'd be Banks or, worse, your own father.

Cold crept slowly through him, icy as a glacier, bringing with it that terrible restlessness and impatience. The need to move, to get away from what was hurting him, and he'd pushed himself up from the sofa before he was fully aware of what he was doing.

Zoe's steady gaze followed him, but she didn't move. There was something calmer about her, as if she'd found strength from somewhere.

'And I love you still,' she said. 'I have always loved you.'

'Why?' he demanded abruptly. 'Why on earth would you love someone like me?'

'Because you're brilliant, passionate and kind,' she said without missing a beat. 'You're protective and funny, and I trust you more than I have trusted anyone else in my entire life.'

The words, and the look in her eyes, the belief she had in him, took his breath away.

'Zoe,' he said, 'I'm not that boy any more, you know that, don't you?'

She didn't look away from him, sitting small yet indomitable on the sofa. 'I'm not talking about that boy, Demon. I'm talking about the man.'

* * *

Archimedes stood in front of her, his tall figure stiff with tension, his blue eyes blazing with something that looked like pain. She wanted to go to him, put her arms around him, tell him that everything was going to be okay, the way he used to do with her when they were kids, but she knew that touching him right now would be a mistake.

Telling him she loved him was probably a mistake, but it was too late now, she'd said it. The moment she'd seen that stick in the bathroom she'd realised she had to, that she couldn't keep lying to herself or to him any more.

Lying about letting the future take care of itself.

Lying about how being with him for a year was enough.

Lying about wanting nothing more from him.

She'd wanted that baby so badly that it had felt almost impossible to believe that she wasn't pregnant. But there was no denying that test. And she'd managed to hold it together until he'd arrived home, but as soon as he'd asked her what was wrong, she hadn't been able to stop the sting of tears. So she'd told him that she wasn't pregnant, and then she'd seen the fleeting look of disappointment on his face and something had settled inside her.

He'd wanted that baby too, that was clear, but the issue with him was that he couldn't acknowledge it. He'd said that they could try again, but that wasn't an admission, not when he was only saying it in response to her distress.

All this time together, he'd been the one giving small pieces of himself to her, and she hadn't given him anything. She'd held back, too afraid to say the truth in her heart in case she lost him. But she couldn't keep doing that. She couldn't keep being afraid. She had to lay her heart bare to him, find the courage to tell him that she loved him, that she always had and always would, and even if he couldn't reciprocate she would handle it.

She could handle anything.

So she'd said it, and here he was, staring at her as if he couldn't believe it, or rather, didn't want to believe it. And that hurt, she couldn't deny it, but it had felt good to say the words out loud, to acknowledge her own truth, and to tell him exactly what it was about him that made her love him.

He was staring at her as if she'd stabbed him instead of telling him she loved him, but she didn't look away. Didn't pretend she hadn't said it, that she didn't mean it. There was a strength inside her she'd never known she had, the strength of her feelings for him, and that gave her courage.

'But you know what kind of man I am,' he said, almost desperately. 'I'm restless, arrogant, demanding. I gave you no choice about coming with me to Greece and then I dragged you halfway around the world purely so you could be in my bed. There's nothing about any of that that's lovable.'

'Yes,' she said, searching his beloved face, 'I do know what kind of man you are. You're all the things I told you that you were, and all those other things you mentioned, those are facets of you, but not the whole.

You challenge me, Archimedes, you always have. You encourage me to step out of my comfort zone and I love that about you.'

'Zoe—'

'You're exciting to be with, to be around. Your mind is fascinating to me. Your presence electrifies me. You were right, I did need to get away from Banks. I needed to find my own strength, and I've found it.' She took a breath, certainty collecting within her. 'I found it through loving you.'

'I...can't do it,' he said, his voice hoarse. 'I can't give you the same, I told you that. Love is something that—'

'You're afraid of,' she interrupted gently, because that was where all this was coming from, wasn't it? He was afraid. He was so committed to believing himself a villain of sorts, using his own temperament as a reason for all the things he did.

Except she was starting to understand that it wasn't his temperament that was the issue. No, the issue was that though he might tell himself he'd grown up fine without love, he wasn't fine at all. What he was hungry for, what he'd *always* been hungry for, was love, and if ever a man needed love it was Archimedes, her Demon.

He shook his head, raking a restless hand through his hair. 'Perhaps. But it's you I'm afraid for.' He dropped his hand, looking at her. 'There's a reason I was fostered, Zoe. A reason my father never bothered to come looking for me. A reason why Banks let me go, but kept you.'

'Oh?' Zoe said. 'And no doubt it's because of all those flaws you're so worried about, yes?'

'I have reason to be worried.' His eyes glittered with sudden anger. 'My mood changes with the wind, I can't sit still for longer than five minutes, I can't control myself when I need to. I've done so many…terrible things. Do you think any of that will make me a good father? A good husband?'

Her heart ached for him, for what he believed about himself. 'Plenty of people have those very same so-called flaws, and yet they do make good husbands and fathers. I fully believe you can too.'

But he was shaking his head. 'The only reason I haven't slid back down into the place I was years ago, when I woke up on that yacht, is because of my control. And I have to have it. Without it, I become someone you wouldn't even recognise, let alone want to be with.'

'I don't believe that,' she said steadily, letting him see the conviction in her eyes. 'You're stronger than you know, Demon. And I am too. I can help you, if you'll let me.'

He'd gone still, his hair standing up from where he'd raked his fingers through it, his blue eyes fierce with negation, the lines of his face hard and set. 'No, Star,' he said, his voice gone abruptly flat. 'I can't risk it, not with you, because you deserve so much more than anything I can ever give.'

'Demon—'

'No,' he repeated, conviction in the word. 'No, I'm sorry. This has gone on for far longer than it should, and that's my fault. I was too greedy, too selfish, and it's time I stopped being both of those things.' He straightened, steel in his spine. 'You need to go back to Greece, Star. You need to be away from me.'

The Zoe she'd been before would have been devastated by the words, would have felt it like a cut to the heart, and would have struck out in rage. But she wasn't that Zoe any more. She was stronger, surer, and she wasn't angry, because he wasn't trying to hurt her, she understood that. He was an animal in a trap clawing at anything within reach, trying to escape. In which case she needed to be calm and patient. Because she wasn't leaving, no matter what he said. Everyone else had left him, but she wasn't going to. She never would.

So she said, 'No, I don't.'

Archimedes blinked. 'What do you mean?'

'I mean, I don't need to be away from you, and I'm not going back to Greece.'

'Zoe—'

'No, Demon,' she interrupted steadily. 'I'm not going anywhere.'

'But I told you. It's impossible for me to give you what you need.'

'I don't care,' she said, staring into his eyes so he could see the truth. 'I don't need anything but to stay here with you.'

A rising fury flickered in his blue gaze. 'You wanted a family, Zoe,' he said insistently. 'Staying here will mean you won't get one, because I won't allow you to be with anyone else. Do you understand that?'

'I do,' she said. 'But that's okay. I don't want a family with anyone else but you.'

A muscle leapt in his jaw and he stepped up to her

suddenly, getting in her face, towering over her. She only tipped her head back and looked up at him, meeting his furious gaze, refusing to be intimidated.

'You really want to stay with someone as jealous and possessive as I am?' he demanded. 'I'll make your life a living hell.'

'No, you won't,' she said, and she believed it utterly.

'You can't give up the chance for a family,' he said, more desperation entering his voice. 'I won't let you.'

'I can give up whatever I want, and you can't tell me what to do.' She reached up and touched his jaw, feeling the prickle of his whiskers beneath her fingertips. 'I'm not leaving you, Demon. And you can't make me.'

He jerked away from her touch as if she'd burned him and took a step back. 'Then you've left me no choice. I'll be the one to go.'

He was trying to push her away, she could see that. But she'd never let anyone push her around and she wasn't about to start now.

'Okay,' she said. 'If you want to run away, that's fine. I'll just wait for you to come back.'

That muscle in his jaw jumped again. 'I'm not running away.'

A deep feeling of peace was moving through her, because she could see him now, the boy she'd once known. The livewire who'd shocked her awake, who'd brought joy into her life, who'd protected her, cared about her. The boy too terrified to let anyone in.

'It's okay to be scared,' she said. 'That's what you used to tell me, remember? When you pushed me out of my comfort zone, challenging me to do something different and unfamiliar.'

'Star—'

'I dare you.' She met his gaze. This was his comfort zone, wasn't it? His belief that he wasn't able to love. Which meant it was her turn to push him out of it. 'That's what you used to tell me when we were kids. So now it's my turn. I dare you, Archimedes Athineos, to let yourself be loved. And I dare you to love me in return.'

His chin came up at that, his whole body going tense.

He'd never been one to refuse a direct challenge and she knew it. But she also knew that this challenge was one he'd never faced before, and he'd probably falter at the last hurdle. But that was okay. She'd wait here until he was ready. She'd always be here, waiting for him.

Archimedes stared at her for one long minute.

Then he turned and walked out of the door.

CHAPTER TWELVE

ARCHIMEDES TOLD HIS driver to wait, then got out of the car, slamming the door behind him, before striding up the overgrown path to Banks's front door. He'd been back in London for a couple of weeks now, and finally had some time in his schedule to demand that he and Zoe be released from the ridiculous contracts he'd made them sign. That he wanted the information Banks had on him and he wasn't going to take no for an answer.

He'd left Italy the night Zoe had told him she loved him. He'd had to. He didn't trust himself around her, didn't trust the urge to throw his control into the furnace and let it burn. Also, her calm acceptance of the fact that he'd never love her, that if she stayed with him he'd never let her have a family or fall in love with someone else ever, infuriated him. That she'd throw her chance for happiness away on someone who'd only keep her caged was intolerable. Her steady belief in him was also intolerable. She didn't know him the way she thought, because she'd never seen him at his worst. And he wasn't about to show her. She didn't deserve that.

Still, if she wouldn't leave, he'd have to, and so he

had. He'd flown to Singapore that night, then on to a meeting in Melbourne, and from there to LA. He'd tried not to think about her. Tried not to think about the lack of her in his bed every night and the lack of her smile. Her wit. Her teasing. Her silver gaze glittering up at him as she lay in his arms. His North Star.

He'd tried a few times to call in lovers, but as soon as they'd arrived, he didn't want them. He was constantly hard but not for them. His body knew what it wanted and he hated that it did.

He wished he could completely ignore her presence, but that was impossible so he'd assigned an employee to inform him of her whereabouts, and to contact him if she wasn't okay. Not that he'd needed to be informed, not when she'd started sending him fridge magnets from every place she visited. It seemed as if she was going on a tour of all his residences in various countries since the magnets came from every town where he had a house, and every time he received one it felt like a knife in his heart. He wanted to throw them away, but he just couldn't bring himself to do it, putting them in a drawer in his London office instead. Really, he should forbid her to visit any of his houses, but he had a feeling she'd find a way around any obstacles he put in her way. She was, after all, very good at getting through security.

All he could do was pretend she wasn't in his life any more, which was surprisingly hard to do. Especially now, back here in London, at the house where Banks had brought him up.

He hammered on the front door until the old man

pulled it open. Banks's craggy face broke into a smile. 'Dear boy! Have you come to bring me good news?'

'No,' Archimedes said curtly, and stepped inside without being asked, making the old man have to take a few steps back.

Banks's eyes widened slightly as Archimedes kicked the door shut, but his smile remained, betraying nothing. 'Then to what do I owe the pleasure?'

His fake cheer grated on Archimedes's raw nerves. 'I want the evidence you have on me,' he said. 'And I want it now.'

Banks nodded as if he'd merely asked for a cup of tea. 'I see. Breaking your contract already, lad?'

'Not just mine,' he snapped. 'I want you to leave Zoe out of it as well. She will not be giving any of her children to you.'

Banks eyed him. 'Why not? Has she changed her mind?'

'We both have,' Archimedes said.

'So, she's not pregnant?'

'No, and she won't be. Not by me at least.'

An expression ghosted over the old man's face, but it was gone too fast for him to read it.

'I could release that evidence on you,' Banks said. 'You'd go to jail.'

Archimedes drew himself up to his full height. 'Do it then. It's probably beyond time for me to take responsibility for my actions. But again, Zoe will not be part of this.'

The old man stared at him a long moment. Then he said, 'I really thought it would work.'

'You thought what would work?'

'Forcing you and Zoe to meet again, to live together. To marry each other.'

It felt as if Banks had emptied a bucket of ice water over his head.

'What?' he demanded. 'What the hell are you talking about?'

Banks sighed. 'I knew where you were going when you left me years ago,' he said. 'I have people everywhere who tell me things. That's why I forbade you to take Zoe. She was too young and I didn't want her getting caught up in whatever you were doing.'

Archimedes said nothing, staring at him.

'But she was miserable after you left, and she remained so, and I realised that what she felt for you wasn't a crush. So, I waited until you'd finished working for the Russians, waited for you to get on the straight and narrow, to become worthy of her, and you did.'

Archimedes could not think of a single thing to say. His mind had gone utterly blank. He'd always known Banks was a master manipulator but he'd never guessed *this*.

'You…fixed all of this?' he asked. 'You made us marry each other and told us you wanted our child because…why?'

'Because she loves you, Archimedes,' Banks said, and there was no hint of his fake cheer now. 'And she wants a family. She stayed with me for far too long because she's so bloody loyal, even after I told her to go. This was the only option.'

Through his shock, anger was starting to rise. 'You fucking manipulated us?'

'Not manipulated,' Banks said carefully. 'More like…forcing proximity. I wanted you two to meet as adults and work things out.' He tilted his head. 'You were always meant to be together, even I could see that.'

Archimedes stared at the man who'd brought him up. The man who'd taken him in and taught him how to steal, to use the skills he had to made him the man he was now.

'But we can't be together,' he said, fighting his fury.

Banks frowned. 'Why on earth not? She's made for you and you for her.'

'No,' he said. 'I'm not worthy of her, no matter what you think. And I never will be.'

'What rot,' Banks said flatly. 'You're a billionaire, Archimedes. You've got a private jet and houses everywhere, so what can't you give her?'

His jaw felt tight, his heart an open wound. 'She loves me and I can't—'

'You love her,' Banks interrupted, and it wasn't a question. 'And don't tell me you don't. You always have. I saw it the moment she walked into that church.'

Archimedes could hear his heart beating in his ears, a dull thumping beat. He loved her? But…no, that couldn't be. He'd never loved anyone in his life, so how would he know?

You idiot. You have *loved someone. You've loved her, and you have since you were a child.*

He wanted to deny it, wanted to tell Banks he was wrong, but the words felt sharp on his tongue, like lies, and he couldn't do it. Because how could he deny her? His North Star? How could he say he didn't love her, when he damn well knew, deep in his shrivelled-up heart, that he did? And that he always had.

'I…' he faltered, not knowing what on earth to say next, the shock of realisation echoing through him.

Banks's bright blue eyes were sharp as needles. 'Takes guts to admit to loving a person,' he said. 'And if she told you, then she's a braver woman than I ever gave her credit for.'

He could see her now, standing in that light, airy salon, telling him all the things she loved about him, which were all the things he hated about himself. Telling him that she wasn't leaving him. And challenging him the way he used to do with her, daring him to pick up her gauntlet.

To let her love him and to love her in return.

'How do you know?' he asked Banks suddenly and sharply. 'How do you know I'm worthy of her?'

The whole world seemed to hang on the old man's answer.

'Are any of us worthy of the love of a good woman?' Banks said. 'But just so you know, I wouldn't have organised that wedding if I didn't think you were worthy of her.'

'It's okay to be scared...'

He could still hear her voice telling him that and his own protesting that he wasn't, that it was her he was afraid for, not himself. But that was just another lie and, he knew, another way to put distance between them. Because the truth was that he *was* scared. He was afraid that the things he hated about himself were things that she would hate too. Except they weren't, were they? She'd told him that those things were what she loved about him…

'She's a better person than I will ever be,' he said hoarsely, as if that would make any difference to the barbed wire that was slowly tightening around his heart, shredding it. How could he have left her like that? When she'd given him everything she was. How could he have lied to her, telling her he couldn't love her? *How?*

She'd always been his North Star. Guiding him home.

'Of course she is,' Banks said serenely. 'But I think you need to tell her that yourself.'

'I can't.' His voice was so rough, broken almost. 'It's too late. I told her that I—'

'Don't be ridiculous,' Banks interrupted for the second time, frowning at him now. 'It's never too late. Go and find her, and for your sake, I hope she accepts your grovel.'

But Archimedes didn't hear those last couple of words.

He'd already gone.

Zoe sat on the sun lounger under an umbrella, enjoying the warm Greek sun. She'd spent a couple of months making a tour of Archimedes's houses around the globe, sending him fridge magnets from each location because she didn't want him thinking she'd abandoned him, but she'd decided that she liked his Greek island villa the best.

She liked being near the sea and it was warm, and she liked the scent of rosemary and lavender. She'd been talking with some of his staff, who pressed olives and made the lovely goat's milk soap, and had been interested in making soap herself, especially experimenting with a few scents she'd been investigating.

What Archimedes was doing, she had no idea. She'd decided that keeping track of him would only hurt her needlessly, so she hadn't. The most important thing was that he knew that she would be here whenever he decided to stop running. And if that involved sending him a small mountain of fridge magnets then so be it.

She'd been fiddling around with testing Ares's firewalls again, wondering if any of his employees would ever find out that she'd installed a backdoor into the software and had been slipping in and out of company files for the past couple of weeks. It seemed very lax that no one had discovered her yet.

Footsteps sounded on the stone flags, coming towards her sun lounger, but she didn't look up. It was probably Lydia asking her what she wanted for lunch.

A shadow fell across her screen and she frowned, finally looking up.

And her heart stopped.

Archimedes stood there, looking as if he hadn't slept

for days, his hair wild, no tie and his shirt buttons undone at his throat.

For long seconds all she could do was stare at him in shock. Then he abruptly leaned down, took her laptop from her lap and laid it on the ground, before hauling her to her feet and into his arms.

Zoe tried to protest. 'Archimedes—'

Only to have his mouth come down on hers in a hungry, hot, desperate kiss. It had been months since she'd seen him. Months since she'd been in his arms, had his mouth on hers, and instantly she melted against him, her hands in his hair, tasting the desperation on his tongue and the need, giving him whatever acknowledgement he wanted from her.

It seemed forever until he finally lifted his head, his gaze a deep, luminous blue. 'I'm sorry,' he said in a raw voice. 'I'm sorry I walked away. You were right. I was afraid. Afraid of not being worthy of you, of not being worth the love you wanted to give me, that the things I hated about myself, all those flaws, were something you'd eventually hate too. But, despite all of that, I'm here now, ready to answer your challenge. I want you to love me, Zoe Athineos. And I want to love you in return.'

Her eyes had filled with sudden tears, her heart inflating like a balloon in her chest. 'You do know that you didn't have to be worthy of me, don't you?' she said huskily. 'I told you, all those things that you hate about yourself, I love. They make you who you are, and you are perfect. You always were.'

His gaze lit, burning like gas flames. 'So are you. You're perfect in every way, and I should have seen what you were much sooner. But I didn't. I'd blinded myself.'

She leaned against him, glorying in the feel of him against her after so many months. 'Why now? What made you change your mind?'

His mouth curved. 'I went to see Banks. To demand he release us both from that ridiculous contract. But… he told me that he'd engineered the whole thing because he thought we should be together.'

Shocked penetrated through the fog of happiness and she could only stare at him. 'What? Seriously?'

'Yes. He told me that you loved me and always had, and that I loved you and always had too.'

Zoe took a little breath, blinking away the tears fiercely. 'So there was no blackmail? He doesn't want a child to bring up?'

'No. He only wanted us to find each other again.'

'The manipulative old bastard,' she said, even though she couldn't be mad at him. Not when he'd engineered this and brought her Demon home to her.

'That's what I said.' His smile deepened. 'But he's right. I have loved you all my life, and I *was* a fool to throw you away. You are a pearl beyond price, Zoe. You're the bravest, most loyal, most intelligent and beautiful woman I've ever known. You're the other half of me, the half I didn't even realise was missing.'

Her throat tightened and she couldn't hold back the tears, so she let them fall.

'Yes,' she said. 'That's what you are to me too.'

His arms tightened around her, holding her close. 'I love you, Zoe. My brilliant, beautiful North Star. Don't you think it's time for you to take me home?'

It was, but luckily, they were already there.

EPILOGUE

The sun was warm, though not hot, which Archimedes was grateful for since he was wearing a suit. The priest had arrived for the vow renewal and they were all waiting on the terrace for the bride to arrive.

Banks was in attendance, a little stiff in his suit, but smiling hugely. They'd had some long conversations with him over the last year, and hatchets had been buried and bridges built. Regardless of how they'd once felt about him, he was the man who'd brought them both up and he was the only family they had. He wasn't the Fagin figure of old, but a changed man. A family man even.

Now, he was cradling Eva, now just six months old, and already ruling the household.

They hadn't wanted anyone else to come, only close family, not that Archimedes cared. As long as she was there, that was all he wanted.

He'd been the one to insist on a vow renewal, since he wanted to marry her 'properly' and Zoe had been happy to agree. She'd been busy with her new company, as well as acting as a consultant with the Ares developers since, apparently, they needed instruction.

Only then Eva had shown up unexpectedly, so they'd had to postpone the ceremony for a bit.

But today was the day, and he was already impatient. That was fine though. Zoe loved it when he was impatient, especially in bed.

He didn't have long to wait, luckily, because suddenly, there she was, in a gown of ivory silk that clung to her figure before billowing out in a flurry of crystal-strewn tulle. Stars sparkled on the bodice, and he'd insisted on the diamond tiara holding her veil in place, worked as a star.

His heart ached and he didn't take his eyes off her as she came towards him, smiling, radiating happiness, glittering like the North Star she was.

He held out a hand and her fingers threaded through his, and they faced the priest.

It had taken them a long time to find each other again, but now they were finally where they were always supposed to be.

Together.

* * * * *

Did Greek's Bride by Blackmail *leave you enthralled? Then don't miss Jackie Ashenden's other dramatic stories!*

King, Enemy, Husband
Christmas Eve Ultimatum
His Heir of Revenge
His Forced Sicilian Bride
Heir with My Enemy

Available now!